The Genesis Game

Volume I

A Dark Dungeon Realm LitRPG

By Wolfe Locke
2nd edition

A Novel of Pandemonium

*This book is dedicated to everyone who helped
me out along the way. You know who you are.*

The Pandemonium Series

Arc I - Rebirth of the Tyrant King

> The Genesis Game: Volume I (Fall/2019)
> The Genesis Game: Volume II (Spring/2020)
> The Genesis Game: Beginnings (Summer/2020)

Arc II – The Dark Lords

> The Skeletal Champion (Winter/2020)
>
> Dungeon of the Old Gods(Summer/2021)
>
> Re: Dark Knight Evolution (Summer/2021)

Arc III - Afterlife

> The Tower of Ruin Volumes 1-7 (Fin/Fall2022)

Arc IV – World of Darkness

> The Hero's Emblem (Winter 2021)

Arc V – Extinction

> March of the Army of Darkness (Spring 2022)
>
> The Madness of Aeon (Fall 2022)

Other Books By The Author

Monster Mage

> Essense Weaver (Spring/2020)
>
> Corridor of Fire (Summer/2021)

Apocalypse Hero

> Apocalypse Hero (Summer/2020)
>
> True John Crusade (Summer/2021)

Netherland: The Owl Eater's Legacy (Winter/2020)

The Hollow Blade (Spring/2021)

The Retired S-Rank Hero – A LitRPG Light Novel

> Volume I (Spring/2021)
>
> Volume II (Summer/2021)

CHAPTER 1: THE BEGINNING OF THE END

The man known as the Black Seraph crashed to the ground. His body skidded along the stone floor as his tattered wings hung bloody from his back, and the myriad of open wounds that covered his body bled freely through the holes and gashes of his shredded armor.

But none of that mattered. He had made it just in time to reach his goal as the boosts from his defensive abilities deactivated, no longer able to offer protection. Every ability was on cooldown, and his mana reserves had been spent during his fight with the Demon Prince of Fire, Adramelech.

His goal close, he needed to hurry before the forces he brought with him failed, their numbers exhausted.

As he picked himself up off the ground, his eyes filled with dark ambition and determination. He looked only forward. He refused to look back at the devastation he had left on the battlefield. He had carved through the forces amassed against him, unleashing wave after wave of power. He refused to look back at the carnage left in the wake of his battle with Adramelech; he could only carve a path forward toward his goal.

He couldn't risk victory for even a second to look and see if any of his vassals or any of his allies had survived. Even a moment of hesitation would be the end of him, allowing the enemies pursuing him the chance to collapse down upon on him, finally overwhelming him.

For Seraph, all that remained was to move forward without hesitation, one step at a time as his life's blood flowed freely from his body, his arms extended toward his goal.

Though he couldn't see how the battle was going in his absence, he could surmise the outcome. With his advanced hearing, Seraph could pick out individual details from the battle. He could make out the sounds of warfare dying down as the men and women who had sworn to serve him died. With every death and every fatal wound, the clang of steel against steel lessened.

One by one, their lives came abruptly to an end; the sound of their death throes was subtle but not impossible for Seraph to pick out, each muttering in the moment of their deaths some wished for Seraph to save them, a belief that he would end the battle.

But it was not to be—though Seraph had promised to deliver victory. He knew the names of all the fallen, just as he knew the names of all who had sworn their allegiance to him, but he felt no remorse, no guilt, and no sorrow, only a determination to continue.

"You did not die in vain," Seraph promised as he forced his damaged body to move the short distance across the ground toward his final goal, leaving a trail of fresh blood behind him. His bloody hand pressed down on the cover of a book that sat upon an altar of white marble, and Seraph knew it to be the Altar of the End. As his hand connected with the book, all the remaining sounds of the surrounding battle immediately faded into nothing, and only white noise remained.

The sounds of monsters consuming the fallen that littered the battlefield had stopped. No more could Seraph hear the gruesome sounds of the murderous feasting—the sound of flesh tearing and bones snapping. This moment marked the beginning of the end.

All for this moment, Seraph thought as he struggled to stand. His hand remained on the Altar as his bloody handprint pressed into the book.

His remaining power channeled into the artifact, his memories, and his essence written and imprinted into the pages of the book, creating in a sense a phylactery by which his memories could be passed on.

Seraph took solace, knowing their trials were finally coming to an end. This was what they had all fought for, what they had come for, and what they died for—his few friends, his allies, his rivals, his vassals, and even his enemies fighting alongside each other under the banner of the guild he had forced them into, the guild named Carrion Crow.

The last vestiges of humanity, a mere handful of warriors, was all that remained of the billions who had once walked the Earth. The few remaining were all great warriors of some renown.

The true elites among elites. Surviving long after the remainder of humanity was long since destroyed and consumed. The strong consumed the weak, and life within the dungeon had been no different.

Seraph and his guildmates had consumed many of those weaker than themselves. Their power was the result of the culmination of decades of building their strength within the dungeon and seizing the strength of those too weak to protect whatever strength they had tried to build. All joining him in this one last battle. All fighting under his guild banner.

A battle that even with their overwhelming power—and the vast resources of the power they wielded between them—was a battle they knew they could not win.

A battle taking place in the deepest pit within the dungeon, the Locum Malificar. The dark heart and final floor of the dungeon whose entrance had long overlooked the rest in dread anticipation, daring all those who would ascend to come and know death while promising survival if but one could claim the Altar.

His guildmates had joined him in that darkest of pits knowing they had no hope of surviving the battle against the vast horde of Ephemeral beings that awaited them—and the army of Eldritch horrors that served them.

Without the hope of survival, they came anyway. Some believed in him, some believed in helping humanity, some hoped for breakthroughs in their own strength, and some were unbelieving of the true danger they faced.

Many more desired an end one way or another. Others still were brought by force or coercion—either they would fight, or they would be consumed in this final battle. There would be no sidelines to safely watch from and hope to be the last one standing. The blight forced them forward.

This had been the last effort of the dying race of men. A refusal to go quietly in the night. One opportunity, the only opportunity, to give one man a chance to end the game into which they had all been conscripted against their will when the world dungeon had appeared on Earth and it's monsters forcefully began taking in people to run its halls and fight the battles within.

This was a chance to give one man, the sum of all men, the opportunity to conquer the dungeon. This chance, this one chance, provided at the cost of their lives in promise that their lives would be renewed.

They all knew the pursuit of victory would cost them their lives. They knew. But to them, the cause was worth that price. Many did not believe they would be resurrected but had hoped with their sacrifice humanity might live on.

Their lives would provide a distraction as they engaged the Ephemeral in battle long enough that the man known as Black Seraph could bypass the majority of the horde and seize the Altar of the End—something that had long been rumored as a way to end the hell in which they all found themselves, and maybe even provide a chance at rebirth for all who had been lost in the dungeon since the beginning.

And yet, the sacrifice was not enough. Even with the battle host comprised of those great warriors, those elites, it was not enough. Seraph had been forced to engage a Prince of Hell, and though he had managed to banish Adramelech to oblivion, he had been mortally wounded, his side torn open, and his heart destroyed.

Though he was dying, Seraph was still able to move by the sheer force of his will and the capabilities of his powerful body, allowing him to evade death for a time.

As he looked at his bloody handprint on the Altar, and as the book placed upon it ceased moving, no longer inscribing, he finally allowed himself to collapse and fall against the Altar, using it for support as his ruined body struggled to soldier on.

Finally, it is done, the monster I made of my-

self has overcome them, he thought as his breathing grew more labored, and his thoughts grew hazier.

Seraph tried to ignore the blood that was pooling beneath him and the cold that was starting to settle into his bones, but he could no longer. The sharp pain that came from his torn wings was constant. Though he did not know what would come next, he was content in his part of it. Content to wait for his reward and the end of the it all. He smiled knowing he would be considered their savior.

As he slumped against the Altar, he closed his eyes, satisfied to finally come to a conclusion and exhausted from his efforts.

Within that exhaustion, everything stopped. Time and space stood still. The remaining white noise that had permeated the air was gone, replaced by a cruel and unusual quiet, devoid of any signs of life. Not even the sound of the beating of his heart or the breath whooshing in his lungs could be heard.

Covered in blood, Seraph would have thought he was dead, if not for the pain in his body. Any doubt he had that he was still alive was suspended when he reached out to touch a droplet of his blood that had fallen from his brow and hung suspended in the air, unmoving.

This was something else, something more he realized as he got up and removed himself from the Altar and waited. He was no longer exhausted, and his wounds while unhealed did not continue to bleed. The thing he was waiting for was coming.

The battlefield that had surrounded the Altar, the site of the final battle of humanity against its total annihilation, had disappeared.

In its place, the battlefield seemed to have given birth to a vast expanse of endless white, and in the middle of that infinite space stood the blood-stained altar. The man who had brought about the end waited for humanity to be given what it had been promised, an end to their struggle and a chance to be reborn. A new Eden to be granted to humanity. A victory. Survival.

"Seraph," said an anguished voice—a voice for whom Seraph could not place the location of its origin. "This thing you have done is no victory. How can there be victory in all this death? Victory was never meant to be the reward, only survival. Your brothers and sisters lay dead on the field where they have fallen, and beneath them, I see the mountains of corpses piled from the innumerable inglorious dead. How can this be?

How could you have failed so spectacularly? I

have promised humanity a new Eden, if only they would reach my Altar, but they are no more. I cannot reverse extinction. I was trying to save you from Wormwood. To prepare you. This thing you have done to yourself … the dead number in the billions … and how many of those billions have been sacrificed on the Altar of your ambition to be stronger. I cannot bring back the dead that you have murdered. I cannot bring back those you have killed."

Furious, Seraph looked around, still not seeing the source of the voice as he raised his arms in anger and summoned a black flame that spread out from him in waves. The flame would burn anything that it touched, and he directed it in all directions, yet the source of the voice remained unharmed. "Why do you do this, Seraph?"

"I know you; I know who you are! Dungeon! Spirit! Monster! Amarath!" shouted Seraph in anger. "Who are you to judge me? How many have you killed? Yet, you dare to judge us for what we have done and had to do when you have trapped us here to play your game, and yet I have won your game. I have conquered your floors, one by one. I have slain your monsters and your minions. It is done, and it is over.

I have reached your Altar and claimed it as my own. I am the last, and no more will come after me. No more will die here to feed the engine of your insatiable appetites. You owe me what you have promised, spirit. You have long promised a new Eden and salvation for humanity, did you not say if only but one would claim the Altar as ours?

I have done this; my hand is imprinted on the book of the Altar. My story is inscribed in its pages. Restore my friends to life as I know you can and let us be free of you."

"I am what I am, human. A Lord of Pandemonium who sought to prepare you for the Calamity to come. You have won nothing. I have long promised since the very first day when I opened my halls that I would provide a new Eden for humanity, if humanity would but reach my Altar.

Humanity is dead, human, and you, not I, have killed them, through your negligence, your apathy, and your contempt. You confused your power, assuming this strength to be your own, yet it is mine. From within my dungeon, you have found this strength. I have extended to you my power, and yet you denied the same to so many others. You have confused my power with your own.

"It is within the halls of my creation you have wandered these many years as you sought refuge from the apocalypse and the calamity that has been unleashed upon the Earth. A calamity I tried to save you from. The blight is not of me. And yet you have denied the same refuge to others. How many people did you condemn to die when the blight overtook the world? Do they number in the thousands or the millions? Innocents whose only offense was that they were weaker than you.

I have every reason to judge you. You who have been petty, you who have been vile, and you who has taken and stolen. You who had the strength to protect the defenseless and the broken and chose not to. You who were known as the Black Seraph, the Angel of Genocide. You who have killed more humans than ever died in my halls."

Seraph roared in anger as dark mana overtook his body, and he took on a terrible visage as he grew many times his size as the darkness made him a veritable avatar of destruction, the power radiating out from him far greater than any he had ever shown before. "You would defy me, dungeon? I am primordial and power incarnate."

"You are nothing," said the Spirit of the Dungeon, and with those words came a power that eclipsed that of what Seraph had just shown. In an instant, his dark mana was stripped away, his body changed into mere vapor, and the wings he had been so proud of were torn from his body until all that remained was the shell of a man underneath.

A man crippled, heavily wounded, and only alive because time had stopped.

"A poor imitation is what you are. I choose you to be the vessel of my power, you are nothing. I am judgment, and my judgment of your kind remains the same. I made the dungeon as a trial—a trial you have failed. A trial your guildmates for whose lives you begged has failed.

I have given humanity every opportunity to overcome their existence, and all I have witnessed has been the suffering you bring upon each other.

"I forced this confrontation with annihilation, and yet humanity refused to do what survival required, which was to raise one another up. To strengthen each other as only iron may sharpen iron, and as only the strong may serve alongside the strong.

Yet, where is your army, you who were once billions? I counted humanity as numerous as the grains of sand along the ocean, but so few among you survived till the end. You numbered in the billions, but only hundreds have survived, and of those hundreds who marched on the Locum Maleficar today, only you, Seraph, remain.

Only you survive, and yet soon you too will be gone to join the others in death when you succumb to these mortal wounds. This is no victory, Seraph. You have doomed yourself. Nobody remains to fight against Aeon, the true enemy."

The man humbled and cowed begged; he could not die like this. "Spirit, dungeon, please, this cannot be how it ends. The others they followed me, they trusted me. It was my idea to hoard power, just as it was my idea that left them all dead on the field.

I thought this would work. We just wanted it to be over and thought that by ending it everything would go back to being as it was. We wanted our lives back. Please, what can I do? Take my life, take everything, but please spare the rest.

They do not deserve this fate. I thought if I took the Altar everything would go back to how it was before the dungeon appeared. I cannot be the last. If you won't revive them, then please just let me die alongside them."

"What is done is done, Seraph, and cannot be undone. But this end is not what I wanted. This is not the ending that anyone wanted. I had not expected humanity to fail in this trial, and I will not allow this story to end with your failure here.

So, to you, I will give what you wish for, a chance that all ask but few ever receive. A chance to go back and right what was wrong, to fix mistakes, and do what needs to be done to save humanity.

"For what is done cannot be undone, but it can be rewritten. As your lifeblood falls to the floor, remember what you have seen and heard.

You cannot save humanity without saving people, and for that, I will send you back in time. Though remember, you cannot save them all, nor should you. Your power will be sealed, and you will return to that fateful day when it all began to descend once more into my dungeon.

I charge you with the task of preparing humanity for what is to come, and to bring them to my Altar. Not you alone, and not your elites. No, bring humanity to my Altar in the thousands and the millions, and only then will you see the Eden that is to come with the fall of Aeon. My dungeon is not your end. It is your beginning and your salvation. Remember this, Seraph."

With a simple motion, the Immortal Amarath restored the flow of time, and with it so too did Seraph's injuries and wounds once more flow with his lifeblood.

The man known as the Black Seraph, but born as Luca, collapsed at the base of the Altar.

His body was finally failing, his abilities unable to heal the massive damage he had received. His wings of blackened steel hung uselessly torn and shredded in two piles away from his body. More blood pooled on the ground from his many wounds.

His power, at last, was failing him, and as he closed his eyes forever, he thought he saw a man made of stars whose body seemed to contain the infinite cosmos reach for him and cradle his broken body as the darkness finally took him into its embrace.

"Three rules, Seraph. Do not take a life unwarranted, do not harm without reason, and all above all else, safeguard humanity and ensure your own survival. You will not get another chance. The contract I once made with you in that fateful cave still applies. You are the key."

Name: Luca Fernandez
Race: Primordial Seraphim
Aliases: Black Seraph, Angel of Genocide, The Accuser, Tyrant, Amarath's Vessel

Passives Abilities
Body of Black Steel
Reflective Aura
Power Incarnate
Charisma of the Overlord
Tyrant's Boon

Abilities
Luminaire – (1849 - 100,000)
Heroic Guard – (12,984 -
1,000,000)
Summon Legendary Monster
(544,000 – 1,000,000)
Glacial Shard (45,058 –
1,000,000)
Liquify (85,480 – 1,000,000)
Purge the Weak (42,490 –
10,000,000)
Hellfire Prison (74,194 –
100,000)
Tri-Elemental Bolt (341
Level: 999 of 999

Unassigned Stat Points: 29
Current Experience: 191,402
of 2,934,000
STR: 7961 **INT:** 3945 **AGI:**
4018
WIS: 5963 **LCK:** 575 **PHY:** 7*
END: 6130 **PER:** 2884
SOL: $194810*

CHAPTER 2:
THE REBIRTH

As Seraph's body died, it disappeared into the floor below it, absorbed and assimilated by the dungeon. As for his spirit, it did not go on toward what dark retribution awaited him. His spirit remained and waited, rather than pass into the darkness, bound in part to the world through the tome on the Altar.

In another time and another life, Luca dreamed. He dreamt of a blood-covered Altar, and on that Altar was set a tome from which deep rolling fog seeped out. A inky blackness that covered the ground and spread all over him with wings of darkness, enfolding him like a second skin. A darkness that threatened to drown him and drown the whole world.

Within that darkness, he learned a truth

of the world that only the dead and dying knew. That to live and breathe is better than any glory or renown you could possibly achieve in this life.

As the darkness enveloped his entire body, he could feel it writhing and moving across his face, smothering him, and as he struggled to breathe, he panicked, realizing he was slowly being suffocated.

In his fear, he could feel a cold sentient and terrible intelligence moving within that darkness. Something hungry for his life, and something hungry with a desire to live again.

Luca screamed in fear—a fear that he would be consumed by that hunger. It was a fatal mistake as he finally lost his battle for control against the darkness that was trying to consume him.

Abruptly his screams cut off as the darkness forced its way into him through his mouth, clogging his voice in his throat. His choking and muffled screams were the only sound to be heard, and as he passed out, visions flashed before his eyes.

In his vision, he saw a man with a face much like his own, but the man was older and heavily scarred with an impossible body that was beautiful in its imperfections, yet twisted and mutilated.

A million hands grabbed onto the man, tearing at him, clinging to him. Hands that could not be seen tore through his flesh and bones as they removed, piece by piece, what had made up the core of his being.

Luca could not look away as morbid fascination took hold. He saw the hands work as the body of his elder self was thoroughly and mechanically dismembered. The cold precision was terrible to behold as the butchering continued.

The body's wings were clipped and torn off, not only from his back, but also from his spirit—in this life, and the next, he no longer would fly, as if those hands belonged to the enemies who feared he might come alive again.

Instinctively, Luca knew what this meant. Those cold hands were not so impartial. The power behind those hands feared the resurrection of the man. Even as a corpse he was feared. He would be crippled and hobbled, his power sealed away, lest he become something far more terrible if he was to rise from the clutches of the grave.

The man had skin that glistened like steel, marred only by the numerous wounds sustained throughout the body. Wounds that no longer bled, the blood thick and blackened in coagulation.

The butchering hands worked quickly as they peeled back and flayed the skin of steel without much effort. In response, as Luca watched, he held his breath and screamed in revulsion as he felt those hands peel the skin, but it was not his. The sensation of pain was there for but a moment, and then it passed while the hands continued their grisly business without hesitation.

The body of the man that had built up to be like a god on Earth was torn apart, piece by piece. Casually dismembered to be used and cataloged. This man, Luca realized, was the version of himself he had long fantasized about growing up to be. Yet, he watched himself be reduced to mere sinews and tendons and nothing more.

A terrible end to the once powerful being, the idol he had made of himself. Luca was conflicted as to the meaning of this vision, and as the images rapidly faded into nothingness, he found no answers. Only darkness awaited, though the dark did nothing to quiet his consciousness and quell his wildly vacillating thoughts.

A voice came to him from within the darkness. A voice beyond space and time. A voice beyond his understanding.

"This is you, Luca. This is what you become. Look at what your desires have wrought. Look at the ways your hands have been stained," said the voice without anger, but rather matter-of-factly if not morose in its robotic delivery. The voice was familiar—like a forgotten memory—but he could not quite place it. It was unrecognizable, and he did not know why.

"Remember what you have done, child. Remember these faults, remember these sins, and learn from them. Grow from them. Do not allow yourself to make the same mistakes again."

A sudden memory came to him, but it confused him for it was not his own. He still remembered the voice. He recognized it as the Spirit of the Dungeon, though he did not know how he remembered visiting the dungeon of this memory or meeting this spirit as he was sure they had never met before.

He knew the memories belonged to someone else. In his mind, he recalled slivers of knowledge about the voice and memories of a life that had never been his.

"I promise I will remember," Luca replied.

The Spirit of the Dungeonresponded, "It is not a promise you can make until you've witnessed who you were. Watch what you have done, dream the dark dreams, and remember what has been forgotten."

As the voice spoke in the dreamscape, an image began to form—images of a memory from a life long-lived, and a flashback to the memory of a bloody handprint on an Altar and the death of the version of himself named Seraph. Though Luca had some more recollection, he knew that he was not him. He was not this Seraph. Those memories belonged to someone else.

In his dreams, he dreamt of hellish green fire that seemed more mist than flame. A fire that both descended to the Earth from the heavens and erupted out of the belly of the abyss. The green fire spread out from each pole, slowly in all directions, consuming all things, and leaving the dungeon for last.

That infernal green fire, that green mist that would come to cover the entirety of the Earth, consumed every nation, every country, and every state. The fire consumed the Earth but did not burn it. From within that green mist, Luca could see gigantic grotesques and rotting abominations moving, the dead and the damned following behind them, straining to be unleashed on the world as they crawled up from the hell beneath and descended from darker realms above.

Mouths ravenous, dripping with saliva, their talons were sharp to rend flesh and cleve muscle. Cruel alien intelligence behind rotting eyes that shone green, these were the Infernals.

Each carried and dragged away every man, woman, and child who had not escaped from that dark storm. They screamed, cried, and sobbed in terror, knowing that only pain and suffering awaited them.

Luca cried out to them, reaching out desperate to save them, but his hands passed through them all. Here he was only a watcher. Tears rolled down his eyes as he could see many had suffered terrible wounds, but he knew they would not die. These monsters that captured them appeared to feed without mercy, but they did not kill most outright. For Luca, this was the fuel of nightmares.

For each person not consumed by those monsters would be taken elsewhere to become just like them. It was theorized but never proven that these unfortunate souls would be transformed through some otherworldly ritual. Everyone who was lost within that mist only made the Infernals stronger.

He watched as people ran to escape the green curtain of death that descended upon them. The masses panicked, aware of the snapping mouths and gnarled hands within that green mist that reached for the slowest and the infirm.

Reaching for those who could not stay ahead of the encroaching darkness. Reaching for the weak and those who had lost the will to save their own lives. Hell descended upon them, and no matter where Luca looked, and no matter how hard he tried to avert his eyes, all he saw was the endless sea of faces frozen in terror.

A shadow flew over him, and as Luca looked up, he saw an older version of himself—the Black Seraph. This version had eyes of the deepest crimson that lacked any hint of human emotion or compassion within its face, aged, weathered, battle hardened and cold.

As Luca watched, the man's eyes glowed red as if to emphasize his inhuman nature. He spread out impossible wings that gleamed of metallic black before flying toward the green mist and then into it. As he went, he called down massive pillars of fire from the heavens unto the Earth, destroying every Infernal that it touched.

He summoned tempestuous winds to keep the mist from spreading faster and grew glacial shards in the streets to impede the movement of the chasing Infernals as they ran onward to overtake the fleeing refugees.

The first of the Infernals reached the flee-ing refugees with clawed hands stretching out, and metallic wings responded in attack. The Black Seraph tore into the Infernals, severing arms and limbs as he attacked. His wings like blades, flayed and ripped flesh while he thrust over and over with his great spear. This was a warrior at home in his element, in the chaos, fighting with fervent resolve—not observing from above—and for a moment, Luca felt pride in this vision of his future self.

This was a fleeting sense of pride that fled once the Black Seraph returned to the skies, and Luca heard an emotionless and cold voice begin to call out to minions and guildmates, point-ing out fleeing refugees from his aerial vantage point.

Choosing who would be saved, and drag-ging them away from their families as they tried to cling together, leaving behind those who had been judged to be too weak to be saved.

As some of his minions dragged away sur-vivors, others followed different commands to work the crowd of fleeing refugees as they fled the green mist. Killing outright those who re-sisted and the sobbing masses, unwilling to let the weak be consumed and transformed by the

Infernals approaching in the dark. It was not out of mercy for the fleeing refugees as cries for mercy went ignored.

This dark visage of himself that Luca had been watching had decided the monsters in the dark were a threat he did not want to strengthen. He would not feed them the weak.

The weak would not join the Infernal horde of Wormwood. He would not allow the weak to interfere with the survival of those strong enough to survive within the dungeon. This was a cold and calculated culling. On those streets, both men and monsters expunged lives in the tens of thousands as the dark curtain of green moved ever forwards.

Luca looked at himself in disappointment, yelling in anger as loudly as he could, "Say something! Do something! This isn't me! This can't be me! You aren't me!" But no matter how hard he tried to get his own attention, he could not stop what had already been set in motion, what had already been done. To his other self, he was just a shadow, an outside observer, and he didn't exist.

Hooded men and women moved among the crowd, their Carrion Crow emblems showing their guild affiliation as they struck down the refugees who had fallen to their knees, unable to get up. Tears ran down Luca's face as he screamed and begged for it to stop.

After hours of watching, unable to interfere and unable to save anyone from the carnage of the bloody spectacle before him, an end unfolded, as the climax of the slaughter was reached.

The massacre ended as the surviving waves of refugees arrived at the dungeon in their vast multitudes. Millions of survivors pouring in from every corner of the world—some recently displaced while many others had fled their homes weeks prior as the infernal mist spread. Every human on Earth. All knowing the last bastion of safety was to be found in the dungeon.

All of the refugees fought against each other, fighting as they tried to push past each other, forcing their way through each other. Walking over empty cars and shattered glass on broken roads and over the broken bodies of those who had simply given up, unable to flee any longer. Those who had succumbed to fatigue, sickness, and terror.

In thick lines and thicker groups, those survivors all started to pour into the maw of the great gate that led into the dungeon. The dungeon that had appeared years before out of the wreckage and ruin of what was once the Mall of Atlanta. Giant and dominating, the entry could be seen for miles.

Seraph, the Angel of Darkness, as his other self was known, descended before the refugees, landing in front of the entrance to the dungeon, and disturbing the dirt beneath him as rock and rubble were thrown in all directions in a minor show of power.

He was to be the final gatekeeper against the flood of wretched humanity. In this moment, he was judgment. Though billions had already died—expired as they fled the dark storm, or been seized by the monsters within the darkness, or killed outright for being judged as weak—millions still remained, straining against the bottleneck to make their way into the dungeon, down into what they perceive as safety.

The multitude, panicking and encumbered by sheer numbers as far as the eye could see, would be caught by the green mist long before they finished moving into the dungeon, and Luca knew they would not be fast enough. He looked back to his other self and knew that he had reached the same conclusion.

A flash of irritation was the first human emotion he had witnessed. Luca saw the dark visage of himself move his hands as tendrils of power spread around his fingers.

Luca recognized what was about to happen

and screamed: "No! Please, don't do it!" But if any-one could hear his cries of protest, they didn't respond or refused to notice, and all he could do was watch in horror at what was unleashed.

A red sludge spread out from those dark hands, low to the ground and hard to see. But Luca saw, and he saw wretched and terrible faces, within the sludge, moving, slithering, and raven-ous. Searching for victims and finding plenty.

The sludge quickly spread out among the crowd of refugees, and as it moved among them, the screams of torment rang out from those who had been judged. Their end was one of excruci-ating pain that seemed to last for an eternity to those who heard it.

It was an advanced spell that used a basic constitution check. A conjured slime monstros-ities to remove those who lacked the strength to begin their journey within the dungeon.

For those who failed that check, their skin began to bubble and fall off as it desiccated from within. Liquefying as the spell moved among the crowd, those who died further fueling the spell, joining those vicious faces trapped in the red sludge, further culling the weak. For every per-son that the sludge passed without harm, five more died. Before the night would finish, the remaining millions would be reduced to thousands.

Luca could only watch in horror as the red sludge moved among the survivors, back toward his other self to be consumed by the man. As the refugees fed the sludge, so too did the sludge feed the Black Seraph, and at that moment, he absorbed the strength of the millions he had decimated.

With his voice amplified by a power, so everyone could hear him, Seraph began to yell into the crowd, "Move faster, or I'll kill more of you. Death comes with that storm, and I won't allow the weak to burden those who want to live. Trample who you need to, push through whom you need to, just move."

The crying continued as the refugees pushed forward, even as the red sludge continued to kill many among them. Seraph may have been a ruthless tyrant, but they knew some safety could be found with him. The dungeon ruled by Seraph was the only safety left remaining.

Multitudes died while fleeing the dark storm, and many more died by Seraph's hand as he unleashed more of his power, summoning a pack of Hellhounds from the abyss to collect those worth saving, with orders to kill all others.

The Hellhounds carried survivors in their great jaws, mauling and mangling the survivors' bodies. It was all justified in Seraph's mind as they would survive—they would heal within a day, and their lost flesh and limbs would regrow. As his hounds worked, so did he. He resumed his purge of the weakest of humanity as his minions and guildmates worked to shelter and contain those they had found worthy of survival in his name.

"This was the darkest of moments," said the voice from before, the voice of the dungeon as the vivid memory Luca had been dreaming started to unravel and fade. "My dungeon was the last bastion of safety on Earth from the ravages of the Aeon's Blight, and you, Luca, killed so many. Yet, you saw it yourself, did you not?

The Infernals can be killed, and if one man's power could kill so many, what about an army? The same Infernals you find on the final floor of my dungeon are the same Infernals that overtook the Earth. My dungeon does not exist to kill all of you, but rather to challenge and help you to grow. Humanity must survive, Luca. Remember this."

Luca nodded in understanding. What he had seen, those images overwhelmed him, and as the dream faded, he was thankful but exhausted from the ordeal of what he had seen.

The dreams were not yet over as he saw himself barely older than he was now—maybe a few years into the future if that. His skin was glistening like iron, with wings of black silk. He was powerful, but not quite as powerful as that other version of himself.

He watched as this version began to kill bound prisoners outside a burning guild hall as he held their guild standard in his hands like a trophy. The guild leader's head was impaled on the standard, his face a permanent fixture ask of shock and terror.

In his cruelty, his shadow-self cast a spell to prevent the head from decaying, and then another to trap the spirit of the deceased guild leader into the severed head to prevent him from passing on to the next life.

As for the guild members, Seraph remorselessly ignored their pleas for mercy as, one by one, he killed his captured enemies, consuming most of their power as he did. He didn't just take their power.

He consumed their souls and destroyed their spirits. As his enemies passed into the void of oblivion, he grew stronger with every kill. Seraph—in his cold and remorseless voice—spoke, resolute, determined, and angered: "If you will not serve me in life, you will serve me in death."

The scene Luca had just watched unfold then faded to black, only to be replaced by another memory of something yet to occur. This time he saw himself as he currently was, a near mirror image of himself, laid out on the ground and unable to move from the shadow of the gate of entry into the dungeon.

A dungeon whose birth had destroyed the grounds it had been birthed upon. Signs for sales could still be seen hanging off jagged rocks and rebar that protruded out from the great doorway that had torn and created itself from the Earth.

Luca saw himself at his lowest moment, wearing clothes familiar to him. Weak, orphaned, desperate, and crippled. He saw his body fall through the air after being thrown through the dungeon gate by a a pair of scared men-hoping to appease whatever dread deity they thought controlled the dungeon.

"Please accept this sacrifice and spare us, Lord." Luca thought he heard the men say as they ran away, unable to look their victim in the eye or say his name in regret as they attempted to trade his life for their own.

As for him, he lay bound and alone in the

dark of the dungeon's entrance. Shivering in fear and waiting for death, his blood poured from numerous wounds throughout his body as bones protruded, stabbing through his skin after being thrown. This version of himself knew agony.

Unable to move and dying, he begged for vengeance against those who had wronged him. He cared nothing for justice—only the power to never be weak again. From within the dungeon, his cries for help were answered. He would have his vengeance. Pain shot through his body as black wings began to grow through the skin of his back. The pain was nothing compared to the pain of being helpless, and even that pain soon became pleasurable as he grew in power.

Luca watched himself become the monster he had seen in his dreams.

"I won't let this come to pass; I promise, spirit. But how can I change the future?"

The Spirit of the Dungeon answered, "I will help you; I will guide you in a way that I have never helped anyone in any world I have visited before. In you, I will have a tool to save humanity. I release you back to your world. Think on what you have seen and what trials await you. Do not forget what I have shown you."

As the presence of the dungeon spirit left,

Luca found himself alone, and as the vision ended, he felt his heart begin to pound as the hair stood up on his arms and the back of his neck.

He found himself in a nightmare, his hand pressed against a bloody handprint, looking at a new visage of himself—a visage comprised of shadow, terrifying and monstrous. However, rather than him watching that visage, the visage watched him. The nightmare was keenly aware of his existence—a fact that terrified Luca.

Luca tried to run, but black wings beat down upon him as he tried to turn away from the monstrous sight of this dark avatar. An avatar of broken black steel wings that had been shredded. A body covered in coagulated blood and grime. Bloodshot eyes bore into Luca, staring into him with desperate hunger.

As Luca tried to will himself awake, this horrible image of himself shot out a bloodied talon that tore through his chest and pierced his heart. He watched with a mouth unable to scream as his heart was torn from his body, and that image of himself consumed it.

CHAPTER 3: BACK TO THE PAST

The feeling of movement woke Seraph from his slumber as tires beat against a paved asphalt. Groggy and tired, Seraph strained to open his eyes. Heavy with sleep and struggling to awaken, he tried to stand, but as his body shifted to match the movement beneath it, he felt something strain against his chest.

Restraints? he thought. *Me? Who would dare to restrain me? What is this? Another trick of the dungeon?* His sudden irritation and anger flooded his body with chemicals, and his body responded by banishing the last vestiges of sleep. He opened his eyes, words of power on his lips, ready to unleash devastation and destruction on his captors. In the back of his mind, he wondered where he was as he could not clearly recall his memories after talking to the dungeon spirit. To him, much of the recent past was a blur.

With eyes open, he looked around in startled confusion and saw that the strap across his chest was not some torture device, but rather a seat belt—a device no longer familiar to him. Light filtered and shone through the window that he saw in his peripherals.

A window, he thought in awe as he turned to look. Through that window, he saw cars passing by in a blurry haze as they sped down the road in the long procession of people trying to beat the afternoon traffic. The spells he had been prepared to unleash dropped from his mind as he took in the moment and the novelty of it all.

Seraph hadn't seen a car in decades—not since they had abandoned the Earth entirely and retreated into the dungeon. But even before then, after he went into the dungeon, he had rarely returned to the surface. The sole exception was his travels preceding the great calamity of the green fire that overtook the Earth and his efforts to root out the enclaves of survivors and forcefully evacuate the talented and strong among them.

Just to be sure, he reached out to touch the glass, the window feeling cold against his fingers. The reflection of a pre-teen on the cusp of manhood looking back at him with blue eyes. A tangled mess of unkempt and greasy brown hair. Despite himself, he couldn't help but stare in amazement. As he stared out the window, his memories came rushing back to him as he smiled, thinking, *I'm no prisoner. It worked. I've replaced my younger self and traveled to the past. This is my rebirth.* The dungeon had meant to give his younger self his memories, but Seraph had refused to die, his soul lingering. He had instead used that chain of events to partially consume his younger self and replace him.

He banished the wonderment from his mind. This was not the time to get distracted. This was the day the dungeon would first appear —day 0—and he needed to get to the dungeon and receive the spoils reserved for those who went first. Thankfully, he was already traveling in a car. It was just a matter of rerouting the driver.

I'm in a car, but who's driving? he asked himself as he looked forward toward the driver, trying to catch identifying details through the rearview mirror. From what he could see, an older man was driving, a salt and pepper mid fade, but from this angle, he couldn't make out any other details. Not willing to put it to chance, Seraph moved his fingers in discrete patterns to cast an identification spell that would feed him details of the driver, but the spell failed without even a notification to alert him explaining why it had failed.

Not to be deterred, he tensed his wings, ready to defend himself, ready to kill the man at the slightest provocation. He prepared himself to launch a quick counterattack that would behead the man if Seraph sensed any intention to attack while activating his defensive abilities that made him all but vulnerable to harm as he sought to control and anticipate every avenue of defense. Yet the uncomfortable sensation of fear crept in as his body failed to respond, and his abilities failed to work. Try as he might, nothing happened. He had a phantom sense of memory of a part of his body that no longer existed. His body tensed in rage as he realized he no longer had his black wings.

Seraph's movements must have alerted the driver as the man turned around to face him, a familiar face with hazel eyes that Seraph could not quite place.

"Hey, kiddo. Was hoping if I left you alone, you'd settle down and fall back to sleep. You could use it. I know you had a rough night last night; I heard you crying in your sleep." After a few brief moments, he continued, "It doesn't help that the school asks so much of you, as if you weren't already exhausted enough with everything that's going on. But we still got a little while before we get home, so why not try to get some more sleep? It'd be good for you to be nice and refreshed before we dig into your homework later."

Seraph felt a sense of unease as he struggled with how to respond, his thoughts awkward, confused, and disoriented. Though he was no longer sleepy, he knew his mind had grown foggy, lacking the mental clarity he had been accustomed to. His thoughts were now jumbled and without focus, in a way he could not remember ever being. This was different from some sort of debuff; he was slower in every sense. The answer came soon enough.

Seraph realized he was normal again. An average, normal human, weak and pathetic. He truly had taken the place of his younger self when he had consumed him.

He needed to get his bearings and try to navigate the situation toward his goals without alerting the driver that he should have cause for concern.

"Where are we?" he asked, ignoring the driver's comments, focused instead on his mission and his goals, a hint of arrogance showing through in his voice.

The driver bristled at the rudeness, and Seraph internally chided himself for the mistake.

The driver adjusted the mirror to get a better look at Seraph and responded, "Well, kiddo, I know you had a rough day today, but you seem to have forgotten that when I ask you something, I expect an answer."

"I'll go ahead and answer that question and give you some time to rethink this newfound attitude you seem to want to give me. We're stuck. We've been stuck in pretty bad traffic on I-85. I've been listening to the radio trying to figure out what's the holdup, but there doesn't seem to be many details for the slowdown. Maybe it is something to do with that freak storm that popped up a little while ago while you were sleeping. Or it's probably another waste spill outside the carpet factory. Not that it matters much. The GPS is lit up red for miles, and I'm not pulling any detours off the GPS."

Wait? thought Seraph. *Kiddo? Kiddo?* He caught glimpses of his reflection in the driver's mirror and turned to get a better look at himself in the window. Something he had not thought to do before.

His body felt different, alien, and unfamiliar. It did not respond with the precision of training and the strength he was used to. There was no sign of age at all. In his reflection, he saw a teen of maybe 15 and knew from his reflection that he was basically a child.

Realization set in that if he was wearing the body of his younger self, that would make the driver, the man upfront that had called him kiddo, his father—a man who had been dead to him for decades.

Warning bells went off in Seraph's head as he realized the implications of his situation. For all practical purposes, he was without power. He would be unable to leverage death, danger, or threat of violence to force others into action for the foreseeable future. If he was truly a teen again and this man his father, then his father was an obstacle that he would have to overcome to reach the dungeon. An obstacle whose only answer was acting and diplomacy.

Remembering the words imparted to him of "No second chances," Seraph knew he had to succeed in every opportunity. He wouldn't be allowed to fail again. He needed to convince his father to take him to the Mall, so he could begin his search for the budding entrance to the dungeons.

"Dad," he said—the word long since unfamiliar, stumbling out of his mouth awkwardly —"What day is it?" Seraph just needed to verify. If his father was unwilling to take him, he would need to resort to force, but he did not want to revert to that as his first option. His success, if he was forced to take that route, was far from guaranteed.

"Wow, kiddo." The man laughed. "That was some nap, wasn't it? You're still pretty groggy, I'm sure. You always sleep hard like that. "

"Sorry, Dad," Seraph replied, the words coming out unfamiliar and with forced casualness. Father was too formal of a word, and as he talked to the man, it seemed to pry loose memories. He remembered his dad never being overly formal. It was one of the few memories of his father.

The last thing Seraph wanted was for this man to interfere directly or indirectly with his plans. "What day is it though, Dad? There is something I've been looking forward to, and I think today is the day." He needed to know for sure what day it was, and if the man refused to take him where he needed, he would take the car by force, even if it meant costing the man his life.

Grinning, the man turned around and looked at him, "Tuesday, kiddo. It's Tuesday the 7th, in this the two thousand and twentieth year of our Lord."

The man waited for Seraph to laugh, his smile turning to a frown when he didn't elicit a response of either a laugh or smile from Seraph.

"Luca," he said, completely reading the situation wrong, "I know things have been hard on you ever since your mom passed, but you have to let me in. We're a family, you know. We're all each other have, and I'm always going to be there for you, just like I promised your mom."

For a moment, shock filled Seraph's body as he was reminded that he had forgotten his own name. It was something discarded and thrown away, alongside his bonds to family once he assumed his identity as Seraph. He found the thought that he had not always been Seraph to be uncomfortable. Oddly enough, he felt his eyes water at the mention of his mother, and he quickly wiped it away.

Seraph got what he wanted from the conversation; he knew what day it was. Today was the day the dungeon opened, the day it first appeared, and the day it let in the first souls who would walk its halls and claim its power. Today was the day the dungeon would begin to unleash monsters in the surrounding area. Today was the day in the past when he had originally lost his father, killed by a monster while stuck on the highway, stuck in traffic that seemed to never end.

He had to think quickly. The entrance to the dungeon had first appeared in the food court at the mall downtown, not far from where they currently were. He knew that the first ones to enter the dungeon would receive abilities and classes beyond what was made available to those who came later.

Additionally, something they had learned in his other time was that the world grew more dangerous every time someone entered the dungeon, as a monster was released elsewhere to wander the Earth, maiming and killing all until put down. If he was going to do things differently, he would need to get into the dungeon first, and maybe there would be long term benefits if he could keep his father alive.

Seraph had never needed anyone in the dungeon, but he could always use trustworthy allies. Though he had no problems using the stick and carrot to coerce cooperation, he preferred actual loyalty. He looked at the man and smiled, his mind made-up.

"Sorry, Dad. I didn't mean to worry you. I'm just groggy and have a lot on my mind. You know, I was thinking, since the traffic is so bad, and we haven't done anything in a while, maybe we could pull off the road and head to the mall? I'd like to see this new game shop that opened up. Maybe hit up some food. You know Mom really liked that smoothie place down at the food court."

The man gave a half-smile, "Yeah, she did." Seraph was pleased the man had taken the bait. "Your mom loved that little smoothie bar, everything certified organic and paired with coconut milk. You know she'd tell me, 'Paul, you just have to try this, it's just so good.' I mean, it was never good, but she loved it, and though I wasn't a fan, it made her happy. I don't mind us taking a little detour. It'd be good for us, so let's hit it up."

"Sure, Dad. I'd like that." It seemed Seraph's plan would work, but he was worried. Stuck in the car, he had not been able to test this new body of his to see what his limits would be. He was confident he would be able to deal with whatever threat he might face initially, but he was still very uncomfortable with the uncertainty of it all. He was also uncertain about how to proceed with his father—and what chain of events might be set in motion by altering his fate. Seraph knew that the time his father had left alive was short if he did nothing. This was the day a pack of Hellhounds released from the dungeon would rampage along the highway. His father had been one of their victims, his throat torn out and his body mauled. Even armed with his foreknowledge, Seraph knew he would not be strong enough to fight off the pack.

"How far out are we anyway?" Seraph asked, trying to speed things along.

"Well, kiddo, your mom would have never approved, but since I'm going to be riding the shoulder it should be about 3 minutes, give or take. Normally, I wouldn't do this, but this traffic isn't moving at all. If nothing else we can go browse some shops after we eat and wait for the roads to open up later when traffic has died down. It's a good idea."

Seraph checked the clock on the dash-board. 12:57. He didn't trust his memory to know the exact details, but he was pretty sure the dungeon had appeared sometime after the lunch rush had died down. Not many people had gotten that initial bonus for being the 1st to enter. It wasn't just limited by how many, it was also a limited-time deal.

"Alright, kiddo, we're here," Paul said as he pulled his car into the parking lot. "I'm going to walk around and help you get out, so take it easy, alright?"

Seraph felt anger toward the man. He of all people did not require help. He had fought his way through the dungeon; getting out of a vehicle was nothing for him. "I'm fine, Dad, I'm not a child who needs you to watch over my every move." He angrily swung the door open and let himself out. His legs unresponsive, he landed on the pavement, scraping his hands as he braced his fall.

He had forgotten how frail this body had been. His legs were mere skin and bone, with not an ounce of fat and even less muscle. He was weak and already struggling, and he hadn't even reached the dungeon yet. And then that man. That damnable man stood over him and grabbed him, scooping him up, a mix of concern and sympathy on his face. Neither of which Seraph wanted.

"It's OK; I got you. You have got to be more careful, Luca. I know you hate it, and I hate it for you, but being reckless and angry is only going to get you more hurt," his dad explained.

Seraph looked at him, every cell in his body resentful and angry. The man saw the look and responded sheepishly. "I know you don't like to be reminded, but you're not quite as mobile as you used to be, and you tire out so easily now. Try to look on the bright-side though, kiddo. It wasn't that long ago we would never have been able to do something like this. It's a testament to how good the therapy is that you've been doing. I just wish your mom was still around to see it."

Everything fell into place, and Seraph remembered. The accident. He had been in an accident. He survived it and had all but lost the use of his legs. He survived when his mother didn't. That was it, the secret he had kept hidden in his other life, in the past. He had been like those who he would later condemn to die—weak, broken, and defenseless. Like a mad dog, he had gone out of his way to never be reminded of that. Much to the detriment of those who had been like him. Doing what he could to kill those who reminded him of his previous weakness,

"Alright, Dad," said Seraph, "I'll take it easy, but do you think we can maybe spend most of the day here? I think I'd like to hit up the arcade at the food court. Besides, it's better than having you pushing me around in a wheel chair the whole time."

"Sure," said Paul giving him a sympathetic look. "That's fine. I've got a few bucks on me too. If memory serves, you can pretty much beat anything in an arcade with enough quarters and time. We could even try this new escape room I've seen advertised."

Perfect, thought Seraph. Maybe this wouldn't be impossible, and together they went inside as Seraph looked at all the people moving about their business, shopping and browsing, all unaware of how their lives would soon irrevocably change.

Seraph was unsure as to how much time they had before the dungeon would appear, but knowing it would be soon, he decided to simply enjoy the moment. He knew the years to come would be difficult; he could let himself enjoy this. He did not need to miss out on simple comfort after decades of going without. As he and his father sat down and ate their smoothies, he held no regrets. It would not make him weaker to enjoy this last comfort while any semblance of comfort still existed.

A simple comfort it was, enjoying the frozen treat of mixed berry, coconut milk, and yogurt that had been a favorite of his mother's —a woman who had died years before the emergence of the dungeon, but whose death had still haunted him throughout his life. He had gone so far as to have her body exhumed, and he tried to raise her within the dungeon, but it was all to no avail. He had never stopped missing her.

Memories could be like that, and as he ate in relative silence, contemplating the past and future, he looked at the man who was equally enjoying the moment, and Seraph felt shame for how easily he had considered killing the man. He remembered how that man had once before, in another life, died for him. Maybe this was part of what the dungeon had condemned him for, how easily killing others came to him.

Seraph realized he was making a mistake. He kept referring to him as "the man." But he wasn't just "the man." This man was his father. His name was Paul, he had a past, he was a person, and he was a person who had once mattered deeply to Seraph. But, more importantly, he was a person who would value Seraph in a way no one else could, once he assumed the mantle of the accuser.

Even though decades had passed for him since he had last seen his father, it did not change the fact that in his prior life, his father had been kind to him. It did not change the fact that his father had died protecting him by shielding him with his body from the jaws and claws of the Hellhounds. It was a sacrifice that Seraph had never honored. He would now.

Seraph made up his mind and clenched his fists in determination. If this was to be how this new life began, he would embrace it. He was a son once; he could be a son again. *There are far worse challenges than reconnecting,* he mused. He was committed. From this point forward, he would think of the man as 'father' and he would enjoy these moments while he could. He would enjoy these moments while the man still knew him as the child Luca and not as Seraph.

In remembrance of his past, and thinking of the future he was heading toward, he couldn't help but feel a sense of unease. A knot was building between his shoulder blades as phantom muscles tried to move wings. He was anxious to regain his power.

His father's voice interrupted his thoughts, and in response, he looked directly at him.

"Gotta say, kiddo, this was a good idea of yours. I just wish your mom could be here with us. You know I've been worried about you a lot, but I think you're going to be alright. Let's make a promise that we'll always be a team, OK?"

Seraph frowned, not quite sure how to react. Deciding to try the words he had already committed to in his mind, unfamiliar and ugly, they spilled out of his mouth. "Um, sure. Dad, we're a team."

Paul looked at him with concern, putting his bowl of half-eaten yogurt on the table. Seraph might be unfamiliar with the setting, but he knew when things were serious and paid attention.

"If you're ever feeling down or like you just want to quit," Paul said, "just say you want to come here, no questions asked, and I'll take you. It will be a little promise between you and me to never give up. I will never give up on you, no matter how hard things get. It will be a good reminder that I'll always be there for you. Always."

Seraph shook his head in disagreement. He appreciated the sentiment, but such a promise was only that. "I don't think either of us has much of a say on if you're always going to be there or not, Dad." He had not meant to be somber or ruin the mood, and he was moved by his father's promise, but Seraph knew the promise to be empty.

He had killed too many good men who had made the same promise to their families. Men who had only wanted to protect their loved ones. He could not believe such a promise. But still, this man, his father, just wanted to protect him, and for that, Seraph was grateful.

His father gave a sad smile. "You're right, I don't know, but I can promise you I'll do everything in my power to always be there for you and give you whatever strength I can muster." Paul then flexed his overall small and unimpressive biceps. "That's what I've got these guns for, kiddo."

Seraph laughed, and the laughter surprised him. It had been so long since he had a reason to laugh. He had missed his father. For all his quirks and his overbearing nature, he had been a good man who had always been in his corner, and he hadn't deserved to die like he had, in the way that he did. Seraph had never been able to recover the body for burial.

I won't let you die this time, Seraph promised silently. Shocked by his own feelings. The thought of his father dying again was something Seraph refused to allow.

CHAPTER 4:
SIGN ME UP

Seraph looked over toward the arcade entrance, past the crowds of people enjoying their meals at the food court, and not focusing on the families sitting together or the young couples flirting. He wasn't here for that. He needed to get on the move and into the dungeon, and his father caught the look and read Seraph well enough to know what to do next.

"Well, hey, kiddo," he said, giving Seraph a light punch to the arm. "Enough of the serious stuff. You leave that to me to worry about, alright? You said you wanted to hit up the arcade. Looks like they've got some new stuff we might want to check out, and I," Paul said, laughing as he pulled some coins out of his pocket, "well, I've got quarters. Plenty of them."

Seraph looked over toward the arcade, and what he saw made his heart drop in shock. Right there at the entrance to the arcade, an advertisement poster showing small teams of knights in armor, mages, healers, and archers entering the maw of a great doorway of aged stone and rough timber.

Admonishing himself for getting caught up within the moment, Seraph realized he hadn't done a decent job of checking his environment. Though he had talked his father into bringing him into the mall—so he could be one of the first to enter the dungeon under the guise of playing games in the arcade—he had never intended to actually go into the arcade.

"Enter the Dungeon!" the poster read. **"The adventure starts at 2:00. Sign up now. The prize? Power Everlasting, Wealth Beyond Measure, and Eternal Life!"**

"A little heavy on the theatrics, aren't they?" commented his father in mock disapproval.

Seraph rubbed the bridge of his nose in annoyance. How could he have missed that the dungeon was right here? The entrance was right in front of him, and he hadn't even noticed, even when it was so obvious. He should already be inside. He needed to be inside, though he did take some solace in knowing that it hadn't opened yet.

Though Seraph had been one of the earlier ones to get into the dungeon, he had not been among the very first, and being among the very first had its advantages—this he had learned from others in his past life who had come before him. He had thought the dungeon had originally appeared from within the depths of the wreckage of what had been the mall. The dungeon having displaced and destroyed the already existing structure. Seraph had not known that the dungeon had existed beforehand inside the mall. He had assumed it simply spawned inside the mall and rapidly grew out of it. That it had actually existed in such a fashion was a secret no one had divulged to him.

A game. He would never have guessed that the dungeon would have disguised itself as a game to be played within the mall. It was just something he had never considered. Why would he? The few who had been first into the dungeon had refused to talk about the details of what they encountered and knew—even when threatened with the pain of death.

Seraph knew that sometime in the near future, the dungeon would explode out of this spot and grow, spreading like wildfire through dry underbrush. Eventually, the dungeon entrance would grow to the size of a small town that would draw crowds and people from around the world.

He knew there was only one option at this point: to go forward.

"Hey, Dad," Seraph said, nudging his father and guiding his attention. "Let's check out that dungeon. It will be open soon, and it looks like they accept preregistration."

His father nodded in agreement as they finished the last of their smoothies. Seraph watched him gather up their bowls and toss them in the trash. Before he was even done with the chore, Seraph had taken off toward the arcade, insisting, despite his father's protest, that he could push the wheelchair himself.

The arcade ended up being a little sparse. They were alone except for a few parents rotating kids through a helicopter motion ride and a few awkward teens playing Dance Dance Revolution. Seraph and his father paid them no attention. Though the teens did glare at them, letting Seraph and his dad know their presence was not appreciated.

Regardless of the undue animosity from the other patrons, they continued without issue. Seraph had come for the dungeon. His father thought it to be just a game, but once they started their adventure, everything would change. Seraph briefly considered a hope that things would remain as they were between him and his father but then instantly dismissed it. Things just didn't work like that; things evolved and hardly ever in the ways wanted.

The entrance of the dungeon was surprising to both of them as they passed through a wooden door at the back of the arcade with an obvious sign above it that read "To the Dungeon" and a path in white paint showing the way. If not for the pointed clues and his limited foreknowledge, Seraph would have questioned if maybe this was just a coincidence and not the dungeon at all.

Once inside, they found a basic sanitized waiting area resembling that of a medical clinic with six other people in waiting—all who appeared bored. Obviously, they had already pre-registered. Seraph tried to make eye contact to register faces with his foreknowledge, but all of them refused to so much as look his way. Seraph doubted that any of these people had lived long enough to meet him.

They both approached the check-in counter and rang the bell upon seeing no one waiting to collect payments or working at the counter. It appeared unmanned.

A hooded figure in response to the sound of the bell came through a door Seraph could barely make out behind the counter. Though the figure tried to obscure itself, Seraph could tell just what the figure was.

An elf, and likely female by the way it held its body. He resisted a sneer. In his previous life, the elves had controlled life for the humans within the dungeon. These were not the tree elves of the forest, or the elves of lore that people thought of when they thought of elves. These were something else. A dungeon construct. An imitation of life that few understood, and the last remnants of a destroyed world.

In his past life, when he had ruled with an iron fist and controlled the player killer guild known as Carrion Crow, Seraph had sent out many of the raid teams that decimated the race of elves and took from them the city of Hometown. He had no regrets. Only after the elves had been destroyed was humanity fully able to proceed to the second floor. The elves, like many things, had been an obstacle in his way.

"Good afternoon," said the figure in a polite and friendly way, her smile easy and infectious, cheerful even. "I'm Sadie."

"If you're here to try out the Dungeon on launch day, I'm going to need you to fill out a few liability forms and go through a quick orientation. It's three phases, but I promise it's not terrible," she continued.

"Yes, we want to try out the Dungeon. How much is it? I didn't see a price advertised. It's not too expensive, right?" asked Paul, who seemed to be intensely studying the woman in what he thought was just an elf costume. A look Seraph noticed and disapproved of.

"Opening day promotion, sir. No cost today, but is the young man able to move by himself? We don't allow teams, partners, or families to start together. That would be an unfair advantage you see. Think of this as one of those escape rooms that you might have experienced before," Sadie explained apologetically.

Seraph looked at his father, and his father looked back at him. "You sure you got this, kiddo?" he asked with some trepidation clear in his tone.

"Yes, Dad. I'm sure I'll be fine. I promise I won't try anything crazy, and I'll ask for help if I need it." Seraph hated acting the part of a child, but until he was actually in the Dungeon and able to regain the use of his legs, he would be entirely dependent on his father, and until then, his father could disrupt all of his plans.

"That settles it. I'll go ahead and sign those forms, so we can get started," replied Paul in excitement.

Sadie pushed the papers and a pen across the counter. Paul only vaguely looked at what he was signing, ready to start the adventure and be gone. Even while wearing the hood, Sadie was very obviously female, and that was making Paul uncomfortable. Seraph noticed his father's discomfort, making a mental note of this weakness to rectify or exploit later.

When he was finished signing everything, Paul slid the papers back across the counter. "And... done."

"Great," said Sadie. "Looks like it's all here. The pact is sealed, and you're almost ready to go. Just let me give you your starter kit really quick, then off you go. You're assigned to room 3, and your son is assigned to room 7. Good luck and great adventuring. If you should need anything, remember, my name is Sadie, and I'll be your Dungeon guide when you need one."

"Hey, really quick," asked Paul, "how do I get a set of those?" He pointed at her elvish ears. "Is it part of the costume we get? Are we allowed other racial choices? I'd like to be something other than human."

Seraph looked at his father with raised eyebrows, and Paul shrugged sheepishly and responded, "What? I used to play Dungeons and Dragons. Role-playing as just a human gets boring."

"No problem, sir. When you get to your starting room, you can make cosmetic adjustments from the in-stock prop items," Sadie responded with a smile. "Hope that helps.

"Oh, and here you go," she said as she handed them the starter kits. "Each of these has an Emblem, the Emblem represents a randomly assigned class that you will play through the Dungeon as. Additionally, the kit had a basic olive-colored jumpsuit for you to change into. Anything else that you might need, you'll be given or find along the way."

"Anyways," Sadie continued, "that's it. Just head through the door on my left, your right. Remember your room assignments. They're pretty easy to follow. The doors will be numbered 1 to 8 on the hall, so it's hard to get mixed up."

"Alright, thanks. Anything, in particular, we need to know?" asked Paul.

"They'll cover that in the three phases of the orientation," replied Sadie, turning around and walking away to wherever she had been before being summoned by the bell. Seraph strained his neck to see and thought he saw her step into a room labeled "General Manager."

Paul pushed Seraph down the hall to his starting room. He had insisted on at least walking Seraph to his door and poking his head in, having some measure of parental distrust of new and unfamiliar things. Seraph noticed that Paul appeared to be both relieved and disappointed when he saw it was just a small changing room connected to another room. Satisfied it was safe, Paul turned and looked at his son.

"Alright, big guy. I know you don't need me, but try to remember if you need me don't hesitate—just yell and I'll come running. And don't forget to look through those props they talked about. If I can find anything, I think I want to be a halfling," he stated.

He was sure there was more to the prop selection than just cosmetics, and Seraph was positive that a weak selection like a halfling would have consequences for his father. "Think a little bigger, Dad. Make yourself a titan, a demigod, or maybe just an elf like that girl," he said.

"Oh yeah, good call. Okay, so what do you think our Emblems are going to be? I hope I get a cool class." his father asked, his face alight with excitement.

Seraph looked at his father's starting kit—a parcel with rope binding and a seal of wax. The emblem of a Sword over a Shield on the seal, it was the mark of a hero—a legendary class even among the elites of his previous life. Keeping his father alive was already having benefits.

"Looks like they want you to be a sword and shield guy, Dad," replied Seraph, pointing to the wax seal. He was guessing the wax seal represented the Emblem inside the package.

He looked visibly pleased. "Oh, that's awesome. You know, back in my Army days, I did my fair share of slitting throats and snapping necks," he joked. "So, what did you get?" he asked curiously, glancing at his son's kit.

Seraph laughed a bit and then looked at his package. The seal of the kit was a pair of black wings. His heart stopped, and he froze in excitement. He knew then he would have a chance to reclaim his power.

"What did you get? You're not saying anything," Paul asked nervously.

"I got a set of wings, Dad," replied Seraph, trying to downplay his own excitement.

"Ah. Yeah, that explains it. The long face. I wouldn't want to be stuck with a girls' class either. What does that even mean? Cleric? Healer? Priest? Boring. No offense, Luca, but better you than me." His father laughed as he congratulated himself on having what he thought was the better starting class.

"Alright, kiddo, let's do this. See you on the other side," he added with some finality.

"See you in a few, Dad," replied Seraph, a hint of reservation in his voice.

He paused for a moment before turning around, just in case there was something he needed to say, and he might not get another chance to say it. There was a deep regret that he never got to say goodbye in his other life before his father died.

"See you on the other side." Seraph had meant to say more, but he stopped himself. The words he had wanted to say felt false and not his own. At least, not yet. Seraph resigned himself to live with his regrets. He could not bring himself to say the words now.

As for cosmetics, he knew his wings would come eventually, but in the meantime, until he could unseal his power, it wouldn't hurt to look at what was available.

Seraph grabbed a prop set of white horns that looked more bull than demon, but then realizing he could end up as a Minotaur just as easy as a devil, he opted to replace the ivory horns with something a bit more diabolic. The option to change your race wasn't available to many in the past, and it had not been available to him. The changes to his body in his first life had been the doing of a dark spirit. But in the absence of past advantages, Seraph would use what he had available.

CHAPTER 5:
INTO THE
DUNGEON

When his father left the room and the door shut behind him, Seraph breathed an audible sigh of relief. To an extent, dealing with the man was rather difficult. He found pretending to be a near-helpless teenage boy exhausting. Having even a few moments of respite from the man was already paying off as Seraph examined the demonic horns that he had chosen from the available props. He was 100% positive that his father would have interfered and prevented this selection. While they appeared cheap and completely ridiculous, he was hopeful that the cosmetic selections made would translate into racial selection, complete with bonuses once integrated fully into the dungeon.

His father truly was a good man who meant well, but he also prevented Seraph from acting to the fullest extent that his foreknowledge allowed. In short, the man was a complication, and there were things he needed to do that this father's presence would eventually complicate.

Overall, Seraph assessed his thoughts on the matter as 'confused'. Whether this was due to general nostalgia or the effects of once again having an immature brain—with its poorly defined emotional controls or impulse controls—it was clear to him that the presence of his father had affected both his thinking and decision-making.

While Seraph had enjoyed the presence of his father, and he freely admitted it to himself that he had enjoyed portions of this day, it had still already become a distraction for him. It was an enjoyable distraction, but remained a distraction nonetheless. Any diversions now could have massive consequences for the future. If those distractions came between him and his goal of conquering the dungeon, unsealing his power, and saving humanity, he would have to remove those distractions or remove himself from the presence of those who distracted him.

While the thoughts turned over in his head, he came to conclude a hard truth. The father Seraph had originally known had been dead for decades and long since mourned, but the man he was traveling with was living and breathing. Though it had been thirty years since he had last seen the man, the passage of time had not abated the sense of loss he had felt, and this man... well, this man was still his father.

Regardless of the passage of time or his current sense of fondness for his long-lost father, he had a more pressing concern. So long as he held the body of a child, or rather a pubescent teen, he was at his father's mercy. At the mercy of whatever whims he had and whatever beliefs he held. Seraph realized he would need to act accordingly until he had enough strength to separate—if needed.

Besides, there are benefits to changing the future, Seraph thought, and he examined his new horns. The presence of his father was not all risk. New options existed that didn't before. Seraph was excited about some of the possibilities that would be open to him now that he had access to someone who held the hero emblem, which bestowed access to the Hero class. In his first life, there had been only two Heroes that Seraph knew about. One he had killed with his own hands on the 3rd floor of the dungeon, and the other his guild had hunted down and killed. It was a secondary benefit that Seraph now had a potentially powerful ally that would help ensure his safety until he grew stronger. But more than anything, Seraph was excited about his father remaining alive, and that very human emotion surprised him.

Regardless of whatever thoughts and plans Seraph might have considered for the emblem bearers and their respective classes, there was one thought that drowned them all out, pushing those thoughts aside as the emblem in Seraph's possession pulsated with power, demanding, needing to be his primary concern: The emblem of the Black Seraph. The Angel of Genocide, the Accuser, and the one who would bring test and trial of the weak during man's calamity.

Those black wings on the emblem were unique to his rebirth, for in his other life they had been his own personal sigil, a symbol that spread dread and fear as it claimed absolute power among those few who had been spared by Seraph. The same sigil which was used as the mark of the player killer guild he had formed "Carrion Crow" in the early days within the dungeon, before reorganizing the guild for more generalized command as they grew.

Seraph grabbed the starter kit, and in a painfully complicated and time-consuming process for someone in a wheelchair, he was able to get changed into the olive jumpsuit. He caressed the emblem in his hands, his fingers stroking the wings proved a curiosity in itself as the emblem responded. In his previous life, nothing like it had existed. He was unsure if it had been expressly created by the dungeon to help him to power up, or if it was a portion of his power he had left behind in his ruined body. He quickly dismissed the former. He knew the truth. The emblem was part of him, or at least, part of whom he used to be, and who he could once more become.

The thoughts were in themselves a distraction, and Seraph quickly dismissed them to focus on the present. He was unsure of what was about to happen to progress past the starting room, as no one in the other timeline had ever told him what happened to those who went into the dungeon first. With no other ideas—and when his desire to start didn't manifest in some type of change—he broke the wax seal that had come with his starter kit. As the seal crumbled beneath his hands, he felt the sensation of something passing through him, and he knew on an instinctive level that if he still had his arcane sight, he would have seen trails of magic weaving throughout the room.

The room went completely dark and a screen appeared in front of him and began playing an audio-visual clip with the message being actively captioned on screen by a somewhat comical, cartoon-like man dressed like a caricature of a bard.

This is likely the start of the orientation we were told about, he thought as he stopped what he was doing to focus and listen.

"Greetings and hello, Adventurers!"

"Welcome to Dungeon Quest. The only live-action full-function dungeon delve role-play on Earth, and that's right, you guessed it. You found it here first."

Seraph groaned. This was already absolutely terrible and seemed to be the orientation.

"But before we can get started there are just a couple of things you need to know.

"The first thing is simple. You all start out at Level 1, and as you complete quests, craft items, finish missions, defeat monsters, or even defeat each other, you'll gain experience that will help you level up. As you level up, you'll gain new powers and abilities and boost most of your stats. To check your status, all you need to do is say status screen, or mentally summon your status screen and it will appear in front of you. Be careful where you use this as it pretty much ruins your vision and leaves you very vulnerable.

"Secondly, you'll be getting a spatial pocket that is specific to just you, no one else. This is just a small gift from me for being our new beta testers. This means that every pocket on any outfit you wear connects with your very own pocket dimension to store stuff in. Cool right? I know. If at any time you can't find what you're looking for, just say the word or think really hard about what you want and reach in for it. In case you're wondering, it's impossible for your spatial pocket to fill up, so hoard away.

"Thirdly, if any of you should conquer this dungeon—and the only way to conquer it is to get to the very end and place your hand on this altar that, you guessed it, is called the Altar of the End on the final floor of the dungeon—you get one wish granted for *almost* anything you want. I've been told I need to be specific about that. Others have gotten the wrong idea. Genie rules: No wishes to kill anyone, no wishes to make anyone fall in love with you, and no wishes to bring back the dead.

"Lastly, you'll find that your bodies have undergone a few changes in the last few minutes. No worries. You still have all your equipment, even if things don't quite look the same. Go ahead and look at yourselves. You'll see you're now wearing upgraded gear. Those basic olive-green jumpsuits have been reinforced with leather on the bony prominences. This will offer some minor protection as you start this adventure. Just know, this is only a very minor protection. Be looking to upgrade as soon as you can.

"Oh, and before I forget, this is a forever game. You'll be able to leave and re-enter the dungeon later, after completing the orientation—I mean, after all, this isn't a prison—but if you die here, you die for real. There is no simulation or play-acting. This is real violence, and you will be put into kill or be killed situations. Oh, and lastly, if you do manage to leave the dungeon, if you tell anyone what you've seen here, you'll be killed instantly—regardless of where you are. Hoped you enjoyed orientation, and have fun!"

Quest Granted: Complete every floor of the dungeon and reach the Altar of the End.

REWARD - One Wish.

FAILURE CONDITION: Seize the Altar while the numbers of humans left alive are less than 1 million.

FAILURE CONDITION: The allotted time

of 50 years expires or complete annihilation of the human race

As the presentation ended the screen disappeared, and the room lost all light. Unable to see, Seraph remained still and waited for whatever was to come next. Then, Seraph felt it. The room shifted, and he felt the telltale sign of nausea after teleportation. Seraph figured it was likely that he and the other participants had been transported into an instanced event or location.

But, in the meantime, he wanted to check something.

"Status Screen," said Seraph.

His vision was instantly replaced with graphs and numbers.

Name: Luca Fernandez
Race: Fallen
Aliases: None
Passives Abilities
Body of Mana

Abilities
Thousand Handed 6-1000

Level: 1 of 999	
Unassigned Stat Points: 0	
Current Experience: 1-10	
STR: 1 **INT:** 1 **AGI:** 1	
WIS: 1 **LCK:** 1 **PHY:** 0*	
END: 1 **PER:** 1	
SOL: $00000*	

Seeing the racial change, he quickly grabbed the horns he had been wearing and pulled. no longer were they a cheap cosmetic prop; they had been fused into him. Beneath his fingers, he could feel the power coursing through those horns—power that had yet to be unlocked. Whatever advantages his new race would give him, those advantages appeared to be locked for now.

In the past, he had remained human. This was something that surprised many who had assumed him to be a demon of sorts. He who had been known as the Black Seraph knew something that many did not—that Seraph was a class, not a racial selection. The Accuser, the Angel of Genocide, all those names he had been known as were all due to a class that demanded him to be a trial of humanity, and in the end, though powerful, he had been only human and failed.

Things would be different this time, and while he was unsure of all the perks and consequences of his new race, he was confident in his decision. He caught sight of the flesh on his arms and noticed his skin had turned the palest white. He hoped the changes to how he looked would be little, but there was nothing he could do about it currently. All these changes confirmed it for him —he was in the dungeon.

He wondered how badly his father was currently panicking or if he was adapting quickly to the changes. In his mind, he imagined Paul banging on the walls demanding that somebody let him out, so he could see his son. The thought of Paul complaining to the dungeon amused him, and he gave a shallow laugh at the thought.

"Dismiss," Seraph said. The status screen disappeared, and he regained the use of his eyes. With these kinds of changes, Seraph could see why it would be easy to panic. But it was not the changes that drew his attention. It was the darkness that surrounded him. It was a darkness deep enough that he couldn't make out any of his own features. He couldn't see his own hands as he waved them about his face, nor could he see his surroundings. This was a perfect dark. He thought maybe he should try moving, but he decided against it. He had no idea how the wheelchair would manage and didn't want it getting stuck on something he couldn't see.

Having few options, Seraph chose the one which made the most sense—he waited, keeping his ears focused on any movement from within the dark. As this was orientation, he didn't expect much damage to come from the darkness, at this point, but it was good practice in the fostering of situational awareness that could save his life one day. As his ears strained and made phantom sounds as his senses deafened, a candle lit up in front of him, and then another and another, forming a path he knew he needed to follow. At the end of that path, he saw two chairs and a small table.

He needed to get there. He tried to push himself over in his wheelchair, but the wheels were completely unresponsive, no matter how hard he tried. The wheels would not turn, and the wheelchair would not move.

"Aren't you coming?" asked a voice. Startled, he looked, and now sitting in one of those chairs was the same hooded figure from before. It was the elf that Paul had mistaken for a human actor. The one who was supposed to be his dungeon guide, Sadie. Though he had been straining his ears, focused on listening, he had heard nothing to announce her presence before she revealed herself.

Seraph knew a moment of fear as he struggled with knowing how easily his life could have just been ended. It was a reminder of the weakness of his current state. "I'm having a little trouble with this wheelchair. Give me just a minute and I'll have it all figured out," he replied, trying to downplay his fear and the extent of his handicap.

"You're not going to make it if you don't move. Don't you think it's a little early to die off? Try your best. I mean, you've barely just begun," commented Sadie with that same cheery voice as before, but beneath the cheer, Seraph noted a hint of finality and an edge to her voice. *Maybe not an edge,* thought Seraph, *but a hint.* A hint that the danger started now.

Looking toward the darkness, Seraph could feel a hunger radiate through the impenetrable darkness as, one by one, red eyes opened in the darkness and stared out at him in hunger. They whispered at him in voices too low to be to be heard coherently. The whispers implanting a mental suggestion that he just give up and not struggle. Though the darkness called to him, it did not move. It was most likely a limitation put in place to give him a chance to progress. Effective and sinister, it was a charm-based illusion spell to send the weak to their doom. He would remember this for later and try to recreate it. But as for just quitting and to not struggle against fate, he wouldn't do that. Too much relied on him, and to quit would mean death.

Groaning and frustrated at the situation, he maneuvered himself off his wheelchair and fell heavily to the floor. It wasn't much, but Seraph was concerned about his body's ability to travel the distance—a distance he figured to be around fifty feet or so. Miserably, he dragged himself along that path, pulling himself by pale bony arms that lacked definition, supporting himself with his elbows. He had to stop every few minutes to catch his breath and let his burning muscles rest, before wiping the sweat from his eyes and continuing. He was frustrated that his body was beyond weak. A weakness that he once would have culled in others if he had seen it, further irritated that his racial upgrade did not fix the problem.

It took him almost an hour to move the distance until he was finally within arm's reach of the chair. In that time, the hooded elf had not once turned away or shown judgment. Instead, she had seemed patiently supportive, though no words of encouragement or discouragement had been aimed his way.

"Stand up and take a seat," Sadie said.

Drenched in sweat, he was ready to rest and went to pull himself up.

"Stand up and take your seat. You will not be asked again."

Dumbfounded, he looked up at her in complaint as he readied reiteration of complaint that he couldn't even move due to exhaustion, and as he went to open his mouth, the hackles on the back of his neck stood up, and his arms broke out in goose flesh as an aura of murderous intent began to roll off the elvish woman in waves strong enough to cause the furniture to be thrown aside.

"Yeah, sure. No problem. Just give me a second," Seraph said, realizing he needed to deescalate the situation. It worked, as the murderous aura dissipated but did not altogether disappear. He knew he had to try something, or she would kill him. Bracing himself with his arms, he tried to straighten his body as much as he could currently manage. Closing his eyes, he focused on his energy. The energy that circulated through his arms, his hands, and his torso. In his mind's eye, he saw the energy within his body try to pass into his legs, but it was unable to bypass his middle.

He had an idea. Though he no longer possessed his arcane sight, he knew that magic was still all around him. Though he couldn't see it, he might be able to grab it. He imagined long arms and hands extending out from his soul, grabbing those tendrils of magic and feasting on them, consuming them and forcing that energy to repair his lower body. He knew it was working when he opened his eyes and saw his veins begin to glow blue—the blue glow even shining through the clothes he was wearing. His legs, though, didn't appear to have the same glow. He gritted his teeth and strained his will to a breaking point, summoning more and more hands to grab the tendrils of magic and ambient mana, consuming everything. Sweating, he strained, forcing the mana to circulate through toes, feet, bone, sinew, muscles and tendons that hadn't moved in years. He then forcefully attached the mana he was circulating through his body to integrate with the rest of his body. Instantly, he fell on his face, unable to brace himself any longer as the energy and magic was disbursed back into the room.

NOTIFICATION: Passive Unlocked: Mana Body - So long as the user has not completely depleted their mana pool, they will experience a bonus

+1 to STR, AGI, and END, and any status effects will begin to heal immediately when outside of battle.

NOTIFICATION: You have unlocked the ability "Thousand Hands". Current mastery 6/1000. The user may deploy multiple ethereal arms through their torso.

The Thousand Hands ability was something he was quite interested in. He was pretty sure mastery level related to how many hands he could summon.

In his previous life, he had killed a few people with a similar ability over differences in how each thought humanity should handle the influx of refugees into the dungeon. If he could level it, this could make him an army of one, though he knew it was likely heavily wisdom-focused.

A few short, slow claps broke him from his thoughts. "Now that was unexpected," Sadie said, her hood down and smiling cheerfully. "You could have just stood up. You're in the dungeon now, and physical injuries—no matter how severe or old—will heal so long as you're not dead. Except for loss of limbs, the dungeon will restore a limb if the other is already severed. Now please, sit down. It's time to start phase one of your orientation."

She was right. He should have known that. Being in the dungeon alone repaired damage to the body quickly, if not engaged in combat. In his other life, that small factor had been a chief cause of his death when he had bled out at the Altar of the End; the healing of the dungeon stalled due to nearby enemies. Sheepishly, he sat down in embarrassment. Seraph knew the reason, he had been in a state of shock from being unable to walk, and with his perspective as low as it was, had not noticed the healing magic of the dungeon restoring the use of his legs.

"Let's begin. Let's do your interview, and then we can get you some equipment," she said.

CHAPTER 6:
STARTING POINT

The female elf known as Sadie broke the silence between them first when she removed the hood that had been hanging from her neck like a scarf. Long platinum-white hair revealed itself as it fell forward past her shoulders, no longer tied back behind her head. Without the hood to obscure parts of her face, Seraph was able to take a better measure of her. Her face was illuminated in a pale light against the backdrop of the endless dark void behind her, accenting her features with a hardness not typical of the elves. This hardness contradicted the outgoing persona she had exuded before. Seraph noticed a single scar that marred what would otherwise have been a perfect face, contrasting with her high cheekbones and sharp features that suggested she herself had a cruel nature. The scar left the permanent appearance of an angry scowl.

Sadie noticed him looking, and her eyes flashed in annoyance, resenting the attention. Her eyes focused on him in hyper-vigilance before she spoke. "Rest a minute and catch your breath. This won't work if I can't hear myself think over the sound of you panting like a dog."

Seraph slumped down into the chair as he tried to mentally will himself to be as small and unnoticeable as he could. As he did so, he took advantage of the small comfort of sitting to let his stamina and his pool of mana recover and replenish. *Pathetic*, he thought as he cursed this new body of his and its impulses. He was embarrassed by the assumption that he possessed wandering eyes, and more embarrassed by the weak performance of his body. His journey had only just started, and yet he was already struggling to meet the expectations he set for himself.

He was utterly exhausted; he had exhausted both his stamina and mana stores to a dangerous degree. For many currently in the dungeon, and many who would come later, the exertion may have seemed trivial, but the effort for Seraph had been anything but, due to his low base stats. The effort had almost killed him, although the permanent buff of "Mana Body" had certainly been worth it.

His biggest concern was that someone had

seen him show this weakness. Should his stamina and mana be exhausted, he would revert to his weakened and crippled state. This was a secret he would kill in order to keep safe. But for now, Seraph was forced to dismiss the thoughts from his mind. The elf was currently too far beyond him, and he hoped that she had not realized the implications of what she had seen.

As Seraph waited for his stamina to recover, he took the opportunity to examine and look over his body, He wanted to see what, if any, changes had occurred following the +1 Buff to his STR, AGI, and END after developing the body of mana ability. The buff had helped to fill him out a little, but it had not given him any definition in his extremities or any easily observable growth. This was to be another concern he had not previously had. This body was weak, sickly, and feeble. He worried about his ability to survive, much less thrive in the dungeon with this handicap in place. It had just become apparent to Seraph that this concern needed immediate attention.

Seraph made no assumptions that he would be granted the same buffs he had been given in his first life. He had been extremely lucky in that regard. He had been awarded his legendary class, fully unlocked, within minutes of being placed in the dungeon. The unlocked legendary class had provided him with passive boosts that he exploited ruthlessly. Those buffs had afforded him the equivalent of a 50-level head-start advantage—something that amounted to years' worth of effort. It was a lead he had taken advantage of to ensure that no one could close that gap. It was a promise and a creed he had lived by and would continue to live by. He would do everything he could to widen the gap between him and anyone who could be an enemy.

As Seraph looked over his emaciated body, he resigned himself to a long grind and difficult progress. He would not be able to boost his power like he had before. The spirit of the dungeon would not allow him to pursue such means of getting strong again, and he had no choice but to grow stronger. He was too weak as he was, and his weaknesses would kill him eventually, if he did not overcome them soon. He would have to find other ways to widen the gap between him and those who would eventually follow him, and he would need to find other ways to build his power base.

As Seraph reflected back on the decisions he had made since his rebirth, he noted some concerns that he would need to rectify. The elf seated next to him had already pointed out one of those concerns. Her earlier criticism was correct when pointing out that he could have simply stood up and walked, rather than crawling on his belly like a dying animal. He had overlooked and forgotten the healing power of the dungeon, and the implications of this were not lost on him. This was something he should have known and had forgotten and overlooked.

There was more to this than just casual oversight. This was a mistake, and the Black Seraph didn't make mistakes. But, he realized, this was the issue. He wasn't the Black Seraph—at least, not currently, and maybe never again. His current stats were the lowest they had ever been. Far lower than when he had first been brought to the dungeon in his first life. He considered his low wisdom and intelligence stats and found them to be the likely explanation for his lack of mental acuity.

Regardless of the reason and the explanation, he had made an error. An error that more than warranted the mocking looks and the harsh tone that Sadie had adopted when dealing with him. He promised himself that he would be more careful in the future. That one mistake had nearly cost him his life during a minor challenge. Out of necessity, this had become a learning experience. He would need to temper his expectations for his own outputs now that he possessed a less than ideal body and an immature brain.

A second problem then became clear to him regarding the elf woman, Sadie. She had been more than willing to kill him just a few minutes before, and while some of that willingness to kill was likely part of her function within this tutorial, there had been something more. Seraph recognized that something beneath the surface simmered—something that triggered a blood lust in her that would only be satisfied when he was dead. A hint of that something in the looks of bitter resentment, thinly disguised anger, and of hate, she directed at him. He would need to find the reason behind her hate. But as he looked for signs of those emotions again, hoping to gain insight, they were gone, replaced with the cheery disposition she had held when processing him into the dungeon.

Sadie interrupted his thoughts with a scathing look of contempt. "Are you so important that you've somewhere else that you need to be?"

Seraph went to respond but was cut off before he could say anything.

"You would do well to show more gratitude and humility toward my master and his creations," Sadie said. "He has shown you a great deal of latitude never before given to others, and he has been extremely accommodating toward your condition and your situation, in spite of some of us having reservations toward your qualifications."

Seraph noted the edge to her voice and the pointed nature of her comments. They appeared to suggest that she knew much more about him than she let on. Just how much Seraph was unsure, but he would take precautions regardless. He would need to assume a measure of distrust with her. These unanswered questions lingering around the elf worried Seraph.

Though this was a civil setting, the dungeon could be full of volatile dangers—the sort of danger that comes from other people's ambitions, need for vengeance, pettiness, and grand delusions. Seraph doubted the dungeon would try to kill him or ensnare him in some trap, given their connection, but he was unsure about the dungeon's sentient minions like Sadie.

They may obey the will of the dungeon, and be of the dungeon, but they were not the dungeon and still possessed free will. Seraph would never forget that.

As he finished up the last bit of stamina and mana recovery, he remained on guard, assuming that at any moment Sadie could strike out against him. If so, he would be forced into a life or death battle that he was not prepared enough to win. It reminded him of something he did when vetting new recruits to his old guild by making applicants fight to the death and choosing from among the survivors those who would ascend into the guild, and then he and his officers would consume those that had not been chosen.

Two options were likely. The first option being that this chain of events was set up by the dungeon itself to prepare him to fight the elf as some sort of rite of passage to continue to progress out of the tutorial. His second thought was that he might be forced to fight one of the other early participants. These were the only ways he could think that made sense to foster both early growth and harden the new participants to the harsh realities of the dungeon.

In the other timeline, Seraph had his own method of hardening new participants to the dungeon. When time allowed, new humans were forced to fight each other in Battle Royale arenas as the other adventurers cheered on for the entertainment. Murder was the price of acceptance. His guild had recruited heavily from among the survivors of the practice. His guild under his direction had administered those Free-For-Alls. The practice had heavily boosted the experience and stats of the survivors.

Today's orientation was nothing like the orientations he had held, and he was unsure if that was better or to the detriment of humanity.

The elf moved to grab a set of Tarot cards set nearby, and, with a calm look of icy detachment on her face, she began her task. She set the deck of Tarot cards on the table between the two of them face down and motioned for Seraph to pick ten cards. He complied with the directions, and each time he chose a card she would grab it and expertly place it in an arcane pattern.

The entire process went by quickly. The elf passed neither word nor glance in his direction.

When all ten cards had been selected, she weaved a series of hand motions and whispered words of power he could not hear, signs of mana glowing as the magic worked. The cards responded, illuminating in blue light with traces of the magic Seraph had previously collected when earning his mana body.

As the cards began to glow, the elf leaned forward in her seat, placing both hands over the cards and speaking softly, her voice aimed at the cards as she began to read the spread.

She pulled the first card. "I ask who is this man? The reversed Judgment answers. 'This man is a contradiction. He is full of self-loathing and doubt, unable due to his own arrogance to understand and be aware of his own failings.'"

She held up the Judgment card for Seraph to see and asked, "Tell me, human, and be honest —for I'll know if you're lying to me—if the world as you know it was to end today, who would you save?

Seraph didn't need to stop and consider the question; he had already lived it and responded, "I would save myself."

Without responding to his answer, she pulled the second card. "I ask for what cause must this man struggle? The Hanged Man answers, 'This man's destiny is his doom. He will be a martyr. He will be a sacrifice.'"

She held out the Hanged Man card for Seraph to see and asked, "A great army that you have led is laid to waste. For what reason did they fall?"

Seraph thought of the Locum Malificar, and though the question was a rhetorical one to get him to reflect on his failings as a leader, he had experience to pull from. "Overconfidence," he answered. "Failure is hard to consider when you've only known success on the battlefield. Sometimes you have to be reminded there is always a bigger fish."

She nodded, seeming to appreciate the answer, before pulling the third card. "I ask from where this man comes? The Tower answers. 'This man is a herald; he comes from disaster and calamity on the race of men.'"

She held the Tower card for him to see and asked, "A rival faction has begun to emerge and gain advantage among your allies. How do you respond?

Seraph considered her question for a second and deliberated with himself internally before finding his answer. "You get rid of them. All of them. Every last conspirator, and every last would-be enemy, even if it means biding your time until you can be rid of them all at once, just like in the game of Risk. If you can't wipe the board with an attack against rivals, you leave yourself vulnerable to be destroyed by somebody else."

She frowned but said nothing and pulled the fourth card. "I ask what this man must overcome?" The Four of Cups answers, 'This man must overcome his apathy, for apathy is death, and indifference toward a helping hand will be fatal.'"

She held the Four of Cups up for him to see

and asked, "You look into a mirror, and it reveals your greatest faults. What does it show?"

Seraph thought back on his other life and the decisions he had made. "It shows that the helping hand I have offered has been a tyrant's grip. I have always tried to bear burden myself, even when those burdens have to be shared by others, but I have not done enough to strengthen those who bear them alongside me."

"That sounds a bit like regret," she commented before moving on and pulling the fifth card. "What must this man gain to know victory? The Knight of Cups answers, 'He must gain discernment. Be wary of low hanging fruit. Ask of all easy things, what is the cost?'"

She held up the Knight of Cups for him to see and asked, "A demon you cannot defeat has taken your closest friend, your father, and your lover captive, but you can only save one. Who do you save?"

To Seraph this was an important question that he had long ago answered for himself. "Love and passion are fleeting, and friends can drift apart, but the bonds of blood are forever. I'd save my father."

She pulled the sixth card. "What must this man be warned against? The Five of Swords answers, 'Be wary, lest victory defeat you. Choose battles carefully or risk losing everything. Be wary of forcing one's companions to leave you. One's actions ripple beyond oneself.'"

She held the Five of Swords before him and asked, "Before you is a great weapon. You may use it freely whenever you wish, and no one but you may use it. What do you do with it?"

Too easy, thought Seraph. "I would use this weapon to destroy my enemies, and the threat of its continued use would be a deterrent, allowing me to suppress any dissent against me."

Sadie closed her eyes slowly then blinked, clear disappointment on her face before continuing. She pulled the seventh card. "What effect will others have on this man's victory? The Queen of Swords answers, 'Another will join him of harsh critique and demeanor, to teach and train him but never know him.'"

She held the Queen of Swords for him to see and asked, "You see two creatures, one of dark and one of light, one of bane and one of holy. From which do you draw guidance?"

Seraph considered the question. He had already been a creature of darkness, and he doubted he could learn much from another creature of the dark, but of the light there was plenty he knew he was ignorant of. "I would choose the creature of light, this holy being to draw guidance from. I know what I am not. There is no shame in drawing strength toward my weaknesses."

She pulled the eighth card. "What influence does the past have on the future this man struggles toward? The Ten of Swords answers, 'This man has known absolute defeat and tasted unavoidable calamity. His fate cannot be denied.'"

She held up the Ten of Swords in front of him and asked, "A man, his wife, and the three children they foster are to be evacuated by life raft in the aftermath of a storm, only to be marooned by themselves on a nearby tropical island. However, only three of them may be saved? Whom do you choose to save?"

Without even having to think on the question, Seraph answered, "I choose the strongest among them—those most likely to survive once they reach the island. Without further information on the contrary, I'd assume this to be the two adults and the eldest child. Better one of the children survives than none."

Sadie frowned but had no retort to it. She pulled the ninth card. "To whom does this man owe the future? The Devil answers, 'The future is owed to his own appetites. The voice that traps itself in the throat. He pays homage to that which he desires—vengeance and retribution.'"

She shoved the Devil card in front of him and asked, "The thing you desire most has been stolen from you. What is this desire?"

Seraph answered calmly, "The power to be free of the whims, desires, and the machinations of others. To be something that cannot be controlled or tamed, simply avoided and tolerated, like a typhoon or winter storm.

She pulled the last card. "What is this man's victory? Death answers, 'This man will know an end. New life will be given, and from the ashes, seedlings will spring.'"

She held up the Death card to him to see and asked, "Someone close to you, a trusted lieutenant, has been discovered attempting to betray you at the height of a campaign. A betrayal that would cost you victory. How do you respond?"

To Seraph, the answer was always known. "If they do not serve me in life, they will serve me in death. I'd consume their essence, their soul, and use it for my own power, and if within my means, I would reanimate the corpse and add it to my minions."

When the reading was over, the elf stood and walked away down another path that lit up as she walked. Seraph walked wordlessly behind her, thinking on the meaning behind the cards she had pulled. The meaning of some cards had not been clear to him, while the meaning of others had been painfully obvious, making him wonder if the magic behind the reading was clairvoyant or omniscient or if she was just skilled at guessing at information.

"Where are we going?" he asked curiously. Just the reading itself could be of great benefit to him if he could just figure out the meaning. He had no doubt in their truthfulness.

"We are heading toward Phase II of orientation, which is the start of your actual dungeon experience. In the cards, your fate—as it has been ordained—has been revealed to you, but foreknowledge should not be confused with forearmed. Maybe the words make more sense to you and you'll benefit from them, but regardless, you will not be sent to start your journey defenseless. You will be armed. If you complete Phases II and III, you will gain access to the ability cultivated from the reading."

Notification: Quest - Complete Phase II and Phase III. Upon completion, Seraph will be awarded a personalized ability.

This was welcome news to him. Any advantage or power up was a benefit. "Just how many phases are there?" he asked. "Am I the first to finish?"

The elf turned around and looked at him, eyes probing him, looking for something. Something he could not guess. A faint trace of surprise was barely noticeable on her face. "Seraph, If you're asking about your father in a roundabout way. He lives and is likely to survive the remaining two phases. Only one of you humans have died so far—a woman who refused to remove herself from the starting point. Her mind was unable to accept what it had decided was impossible. She was judged to have forfeited her right to survival, and the dungeon consumed her."

This piqued Seraph's interest. She had been killed not by an environmental threat or an enemy, but by being judged unworthy to live. How was that any different from many of the lives he had taken?

"Why did the dungeon consume her?" Seraph asked, wanting clarity.

"She knew her life was in danger and refused, even in fear of death, to step forward. She had chosen the cosmetics of what you would deem a mermaid and began to asphyxiate without water. She refused the accommodations provided to ensure her survival. We have arrived," she finished.

The dark path had led them to an ornate oak door. Just a door—no walls, and no ceiling —though it was a beautiful door with sculpted bronze and gold leaves. The elf reached into the collar of her clothing and pulled out a key with which to open the door and motioned for him to go inside.

An elven armory, he realized as he stepped through. Inside, he saw racks filled with weapons and armor of all types, neatly packed away in this pocket dimension. Convenient to quickly transport weapons for an army. He had only heard of these armories in his other life, but he had never seen them.

When he had conquered the elves in the

other timeline, he had not been able to secure all the spoils before his few rivals, and special resources like this had been very rare. Rare enough that the other humans had destroyed their armories when they found themselves fearful over losing control of them to Seraph. The key itself held the armory and could be opened from any door.

"What weapon do you have an aptitude with?" asked the elf, though Seraph guessed she already knew the answer. "You need to be taught the basics."

Finally, this was an area were Seraph could show his genius as one of humanity's elites, long-favoring an elegant spear over all other weapons. "The long spear. Give me the long spear.' The elf arched her eyebrows, clearly questioning how sound of a decision that was.

Regardless of her doubt, it was his decision, and he insisted, so she tossed the spear toward him. His fingers barely brushed the shaft of the spear before dropping it on the ground. "Can you at least pick it up and hold it?" He was absolute in his confidence that he could, but the elf had her doubts and made those doubts well known and apparent.

His own doubts appeared after he struggled to pick up the spear, and they worsened when he struggled to hold it, his arms shaking with exertion before being forced to drop it. Even with his mana body buff, he was still too weak to wield the weapon that in his other life he had been an expert with.

The elf looked at him with open contempt. "Part of being a man is knowing one's own limits. It seems you can't recognize yours. What other weaknesses do you have? Too prideful to see and recognize. How could you not have known your limits? I have an easy solution for this. In the absence of good fundamentals, and when lacking proper physicality, a mace will have to do until you are able to pick some skills."

She rolled the mace over to him on the floor. She had a valid point, Seraph had to admit. He wasn't strong enough to wield his weapon of choice—regardless of his experience. He picked up the mace, admiring its simple design and its relatively lightweight, and though he was a pure novice with the weapon, he was confident he would soon be able to master it.

He took a stance and began going through a series of movements to try to get a feel for the weapon. With each movement, the power of the armory was fully transparent as pieces of gear and armor began flying off the racks and shelves, until, finally, the clothes he had been wearing had been reduced to bare thread at his feet, and he found a new outfit being magically put on him. A dusty olive-black overcoat with his soft areas wrapped in a gray cloth under armor, and the shoes he was wearing were replaced by heavy steel-toed tan boot. It offered some more protection for him.

"It originally came with a tweed cap, but it was decided with your new horns it wouldn't do, and with your new racial attributes, it was deemed you needed something thicker than the jumpsuit you were wearing. Fallen are quite susceptible to the cold," explained Sadie.

No sooner had he finished inspecting his new look, when he felt an intense killing intent again. The elf was moving toward him to attack, her hand brandishing a short-curved sword. In his other life, blocking and countering the attack would have been easy. Instead, he was struggling with rare indecision at the worst of times. He made his choice. He was unsure if he could block the attack with his current body, so rather than try, he jumped out of the way as the blade descended.

As he jumped, he heard the sound of a blade slicing through the air but heard nobody shifting, and still, his vision remained on Sadie. Someone or something was attacking him from behind, and without the ability to maneuver in the air, he had no choice but to block as he slammed his mace into the downward slicing sword. As his mace connected with the steel of the blade for a moment, his eyes locked with the pale blue orbs of the Spectral Knight that had attacked him, which disappeared immediately after its blow had been blocked.

"Well done," said the elf in simple compliment. "Two more of you humans died during this iteration. One neither attempted to block the attack nor move out of the way—the fool thought his new-found stature as a Minotaur made him somehow immune to attacks—and the other assumed skill with a blade based on his new Elven stature, skill that he didn't possess. Both have learned a deadly lesson."

That made sense to Seraph. "Learning firsthand is different from being told. It's a valuable experience, though I thought it would be more complicated. All you did was try to attack me and sent your Spectral Knight after me. Besides, what about my father? How did he do?"

"I didn't try to attack you. I loudly broadcast that I would kill you, and I would have if you did less than required to survive, move, or block my attack. I also made sure my minion was loud enough to warn you of the danger. This isn't a trial, it's a tutorial. The intent is to help people live—even if it kills a few. And, yes, your father is fine, though you may be surprised at his changes," said the elf. "Considering how un-impressive your performance was, he's a natural prodigy and a genius with the blade. He actually asked for a long knife, the ceremonial dagger of a calvary soldier, and had to explain a bit to us about what exactly one was."

The elf continued, "And no, human, this wasn't it. This isn't phase two. You remaining humans are going to do a quick run through a trial dungeon allow you to get a feel for what the real one will be like. You'll be given abilities based on your reading to assist you."

The elf pulled out her key again and headed toward the door. "Come on now. It's time for Phase II. This is the fieldwork portion—the trial dungeon."

CHAPTER 7:
PHASE II BEGINS

Seraph followed the dungeon guide as she walked off into the gloom that surrounded them. With his eyesight boosted by his new racial attributes, he had no difficulty keeping up with her in the dark. After they had walked for some time, she held up her hand in a closed fist to get Seraph to stop in place as she pulled another item from her spatial storage and threw it on the ground.

Without any noise, an aged-looking brown door grew up from the spot in which she had thrown the item. She looked back at him as if to say, 'Come along' and opened the door. Though only darkness could be seen within that doorway, she stepped through it without hesitation.

Seraph looked at the door in suspicion; he had reason to hesitate. He had no way of knowing what he would find on the other side until he stepped through the doorway. He didn't hesitate long. The only answer for him was forward, following behind her. As he passed through the doorway, his eyes were temporarily blinded by the sheer light that glared down at him with an intensity he had never struggled with before. He covered his eyes with his hands, trying to shield himself from the white glare and give his vision time to recover.

"Your eyes will get used to it," remarked Sadie. "It's the racial change. I'm sure you've found your eyesight in the dark has dramatically improved. This is a passive trait of all Fallen—you'll find that you're more suited for the dark than the light. Fitting really, considering your background, Seraph."

Notification: Passive Unlocked – Due to your racial change to "Fallen", you have discovered a weakness to light, manifesting as temporary blindness when exposed to light. Alternatively, you have discovered that you now possess "Dark Vision", which grants the user limited vision in the absence of light and increased vision in reduced light environments".

There it is again, thought Seraph as Sadie made yet another comment suggesting she may know his true identity. Seraph couldn't rule out that she still had her memories from the other timeline. He couldn't rule out that all the elves still had their memories from before.

Red flags went off in his head as the realization of the danger he was in hit him. "Blind!" he cursed. "This is the last thing I needed." Seraph almost missed the sound of footsteps running toward him, pounding against the wooden flooring he felt beneath his feet, heading his direction.

In the absence of one of his senses, he knew a method to supplement his other senses, but he could not currently use it due to his low stats. But in this situation, he didn't need better senses to tell him something was going to crash into him. He braced himself for the hit, unable to see what was coming his way and unable to defend himself.

"Can you help me, Sadie?" Seraph asked, assuming the dungeon guide might be responsible for assisting him in this situation.

"I'm just a guide, not a babysitter," she answered in a cheery tone—a tone that no one but Seraph could tell was full of mockery. The message was received; he was on his own.

As the sound of running moved closer to him, Seraph resigned himself for the hit as the impact was upon him. But the hit never came. Instead, Seraph felt hands grab him and pick him up, wrapping him in a long extended hold, threatening to break his ribs. *No, not a hold*, he thought with a sigh of relief. *Just a hug.*

"Kiddo! This is amazing!" said a familiar voice—the voice of his father—and though Seraph's vision was only just now starting to adjust to the bright light, he could make out the biggest smile on his father's face. The man's happiness was evident.

It was a good-natured greeting, and Seraph matched the smile. "It is pretty amazing, as I'm sure you can see for yourself," he said as he tried to bring attention to his legs.

"Yeah, I noticed you're upright and on two legs. I wish your mom could see this. I'm not so sure about the rest of these changes, though. They remind me of when I watched *Powder* with your mom, to be honest, Luca. Is any of that reversible?" he asked, still smiling as he wiped a few tears from his eyes on his outfit. He looked and examined Seraph's new horns, the change in his skin tone, and the darkening of his pupils.

"You know this place really is something," Paul said, quickly changing the subject. Seraph could tell the man was uncomfortable with Seraph no longer being fully human, and Seraph didn't want to spoil the overall mood, so as the subject changed, he went with it.

"It really is something. Everyone is going to get a chance at it," replied Seraph. "But what about you? I was positive you'd be an elf by now. You seemed very interested before. What happened?"

"Well, you know, I wasn't really sure what I wanted to pick. I was mostly afraid of misunderstanding the prop I selected. I didn't want to dress up as like a dragon and end up having to role play as a lizard man. I figured everyone else would want to be an elf, and that's boring. But I do have a surprise. You might be able to walk now, but I can do one better. I can walk on the air."

"Oh, really?" asked Seraph with genuine interest. "How is that? Show me."

With a huge smile on his face, and not waiting for any further prompting, Paul proceeded to jump into the air. It wasn't an impressive jump as such, but rather than fall back down, his feet seemed to catch on something, like a piece of resistance in the air, and he pushed off again, repeating the process before falling back to the ground with a heavy thud.

"A double jump? That's going to be really useful later," said Seraph with envy. Whatever the arena, mobility was always a strength.

"Not quite, kiddo. This isn't a double jump. This is my new passive ability. Here, I'll show you." Seraph wasn't sure what Paul was doing, but he made sure to pay attention in case he had learned something he didn't. Paul seemed to reach out to grab an invisible prompt and threw it toward Seraph. Seraph had never before seen this share-based mechanic, but he did what he thought might be the most appropriate, and he tried to catch it."

PASSIVE Ability - To the Top - The holder of this ability is able to create temporary stairs of air that fade after being stepped on. This is limited to 5 steps + total levels.

"Amazing right?" Paul said and laughed. "I'm assuming since I decided to stay a regular guy, the powers that be decided to give me an ability to make up for it. Aside from a few questionable cosmetic changes, did you get anything else out of your orientation?"

Seraph didn't really want to say he likely wasn't given an ability because of the abilities he had unlocked as a matter of balancing. He didn't want to divulge that he had instead earned the Mana Body passive ability and the Thousand Hands active ability. Information about one's capabilities shouldn't be given so freely.

Seeing his hesitation, Paul lost some of his good humor and frowned, suddenly very concerned. "They didn't do anything weird right, Luca? Or something wrong? I know this is all so unbelievable. I wouldn't believe it if I didn't see it for myself. It's OK to tell me what you got; I promise no judgments here. I'm sure they hooked you up with a good ability."

Seraph looked at his guide for clues on how to react. She only shrugged and put the responsibility back on him. Though what his father had said made sense, it was also hard for Seraph to get an idea of the best course of action to take, and his father wasn't the only one listening. Though he had foreknowledge, his foreknowledge was limited. He had not done this tutorial previously, and with this many changes occurring so quickly, there was no guarantee that his limited foreknowledge could even be useful here.

As for his father... well, the man appeared to have already accepted and adapted to some impossible changes in his life. It was something Seraph felt was unbelievable, and it made him wary of the man. One thing he had always known to be true, and had always proven to be true, was that people changed with power.

Eventually, the pause between them grew awkward, and Seraph continued to not respond. Sadie finally intervened, "The general manager was prepared to offer this boy an ability the same as the rest of you have been provided. However, as I manage Phase I of this tutorial, what you might refer to as the orientation, I have sole discretion on whether he receives anything, and this boy has enough advantages. It's generous enough that we've allowed him to walk again."

Seraph was hardly surprised by the answer. For whatever reason, Sadie had deemed herself to be hostile to him, though he was unsure if she was his enemy as well. But the rage on his father's face in response to her was intense. His hands shook in anger, and his skin turned an obvious shade of red as his blood boiled to match his fury. Paul leveled his finger against the elf woman in accusation, but before it could escalate, a young elvish man pushed past him, getting between Sadie and Paul and trying to prevent the situation from getting out of hand and out of control before anyone did anything they might regret.

This man instinctively knew something that Paul did not. Something that Seraph knew firsthand. This Sadie, the elf who was their guide, was not someone any of them could lay hands on and live to regret later. The elves of the dungeon were currently far beyond them, though Seraph knew this would not always be the case.

"You know that decision isn't right. It's not fair. Would you perhaps reconsider?" asked the elvish man. From around the room, Seraph could see another elvish man and elvish woman nodding their heads in agreement—all familiar faces he had seen during preregistration, and all faces now sporting pointed ears. "We've all got abilities, so why didn't he get anything? Where do you get off on that?"

Ignoring the others, Sadie looked at Paul and said with a tone of pure ice, all traces of her previous upbeat characterization gone, "Be thankful this man saved your fool life. It doesn't matter who you are or what you think you're owed, if you ever think of putting your filthy human hands on me again, I'll cut you down like the animal you are."

Sadie then turned to respond to the man who had asked the question, and as she spoke, she turned to look at Seraph. "It's bad enough how many allowances have been made for a cripple; he needs to prove himself. If he can't manage with what he has at this point, what's the use of pandering to the weakest among you? Right, Seraph? The weak should be culled if they can't rise above it?"

Dismissively, and without waiting for a response, she turned around and opened the door behind her, stepping through it without a second look. She shouted as she went in her cheerful and mocking voice, "Good luck, pretenders!" The doorway she had summoned slammed as she walked through it, closing behind her. As it closed, the doorway began to disappear until nothing remained of it, leaving five new adventurers alone in what appeared to be a high school gymnasium.

Seraph realized as his eyesight finally returned, the light that had blinded him wasn't even the sun. He would need to be careful, and as soon as he could, he would have to find some protection.

"Wow," said the elvish man who had

stepped between Paul and Sadie, "that was just a bit terrifying. I don't know what you did to make her so mad, but without a doubt she hates you. I'd watch your back around her, if you ever see her again. That said, I'm Jack." The man held his hand out to shake with a good-natured smile. "And though we haven't been introduced yet, this is Erin, and that's Alexander," he added, pointing to a woman dressed in a gray smock, who smiled and gave a small wave at Paul and Seraph, and a man with a crew cut wearing an olive jumpsuit.

"I'm not really sure what her deal is either," replied Seraph. "But this is my father, Paul, and I'm Luca. If you followed any of that exchange, I'll admit it right now. Up until today, I was in a wheelchair, and now I'm not. If that seems odd to anyone, let's work out the details now."

"A wheelchair? And now you can walk? That's pretty amazing, but I'm more concerned that you decided to dress up as every emo kid I ever knew growing up whose parents didn't love them enough," commented Erin with a laugh, eliciting a smile from Jack and Alexander. Seraph noticed Paul tried to hide a ghost of a smile on his.

"You think it's like that for everyone who comes in here? Do they get fixed like you did?"

asked Alexander. "Like do people get magically cured by just being here?"

Seraph shrugged. He wasn't really sure. In the other timeline, those who had lost the use of arms and legs regained them once in the dungeon. "It probably depends on what it takes to get somebody into fighting shape. I think that's what this place is all about. Fighting and growing," Seraph responded.

"Alright, that's enough, guys. Let's all circle up for a second and compare notes while we've got a minute," interrupted Jack. "Alexander, you've been here the longest right? Who brought you here?"

Alexander thought for a second. "I think I've been here now for longer than a few hours. If I was to try to pin it down, I'd say I've been here in this gym for five maybe six hours, and it's been almost a full day since I entered the dungeon. That same crazy broad that just left is the same one that first dropped me off here. I've seen her bring and drop off the rest of you guys, just like she did with me.

"That's impossible, though," said Paul. "I only got here a few minutes before my son did —maybe a ten to fifteen-minute max overlap— and I've been in the dungeon now for only a few hours.

"I can see how you would think that, Dad," Seraph said. "But it's been less than an hour for me since I even entered the dungeon, and I'm guessing if we let the other two talk, there's going to be some further time irregularities."

"I can confirm some of that," admitted Jack. "The same elf brought me here, and I saw the same elf bring both Erin and then Paul here, and then Paul's kid."

Jack and Erin both nodded their heads.

"Alright, let's review," said Jack. "So, the time is all sorts of crazy here, and the same person brought all of us here, but our individual perception of time isn't the same. So, I'm guessing each of us was kind of kept in some kind of pocket dimension in like a form of stasis until all of us were ready to begin this stage. Likely, Paul and the kid have been in stasis the longest, and Alexander might not have been in stasis at all. At least, that's my theory. It's only a theory; don't hate me for it. I'm not married to it. Additionally, even though the same elf appeared to take us all, I think we need to be open to the possibility of doppelgängers or even a splitting ability. That might not matter now, but it could later, so do keep it in mind."

Paul shrugged. "I mean, I don't have any better ideas to contradict what you've summed up. It's already been a day full of impossible for me. It would be dumb of me to just discount anything at this point as being unrealistic. I'll just have to toss this one into the magic bucket and let it go. I'd rather not try to get too deep into these things right now to figure out where I draw the believability line."

Seraph couldn't fault that thinking. Many in the other timeline had lost their minds, their sanity broken by the trauma of the impossible existence that was the dungeon.

"Alright, guys, so if this is supposed to be a tutorial dungeon, we should learn a little more about what each of us brings to the table. I'll start," said Jack. "My ability is Chained Necrotic Pet. Basically, if I understand it correctly, I can reanimate a corpse that will follow me around, and any damage I might take, the corpse takes instead. It's a little creepy I know. I'm sorry. I didn't pick it."

Everyone took a subtle step away from Jack after that reveal, except for Seraph who held his position. Seraph was familiar with aspects of the ability; it was extremely useful. It was odd though that Seraph had no memory of Jack from the other timeline.

"Real quick," interjected Alexander, "I know it didn't come up yet, but I've had plenty of time to actually look around in here to see if there was anything to see. Basically, we're all stuck. I've checked all the doors, and each is locked. However, it's like no lock I've ever seen. It's more like a wall that's pretending to be a door than anything."

That sounded accurate to Seraph, but he chose not to say anything.

"Alright, thanks," said Jack dismissively, ignoring the implications that they were effectively trapped until the dungeon decided otherwise.

Fool, thought Seraph in judgment. Knowledge is power, and dismissing what others know is also dismissing revelations on what they are capable of.

"Alright, Erin you're up. We already know Paul's ability, and that the kid doesn't have one. So, what's yours?" asked Jack.

"Um... OK, well my ability is called Starcall, and the prompt said that I can choose a spot, and it will light up like a star for a few seconds, leaving all who look at it blinded," Erin explained as she bit on her fingernails in passive anxiety.

That's a very useful ability, though it's being wasted on someone without any innate talent in combat, thought Seraph as he examined the woman and found no evidence of strength.

Though he knew plenty about this ability, he refused to add to the conversation with his own insight. He didn't want to let on that he knew more than he should. That sort of attention would be detrimental to him and could be a hazard. If he couldn't figure out a way to steal or harness that ability discreetly, he would need to find ways to help her grow and use it. However, if he could steal or harness it, he had no intention of helping her increase her strength with it.

"Alright, Alexander, that leaves just you. What's your ability?" asked Jack, and all eyes turned toward Alexander.

Alexander looked at him, ignoring the question. "My ability doesn't matter. It's not your business, it's mine. If I need to use it, I'll use it, and if I need to use it to help you guys, I'll use it. Otherwise, it's not your concern, and it's not open to discussion."

Jack looked at him pleading. "Come on, man, don't be like that. We are all in this together. If we work together, we have the best chance of getting through this, and that's going to require a little trust from you."

Alexander replied, "Yeah, that's not going to happen. I'm not sure if you noticed, but we started registration with eight of us, and now we're down to five. Little-by-little our group is being whittled down. Does that mean anything, I don't know. But what I do know is that I have an ability I want to keep to myself, and my ability is my trump card if I ever need one—and I'm pretty sure I will need one. Besides, aren't you the one who just mentioned that people here might not be who they seem to be, with all that talk of splicing, clones, and doppelgängers?"

"Fair enough," said Jack, not wanting to push the issue. "I'm not sure what our next step is going to be, but I think we need to choose a leader of our merry band, then find a way out of here. For leaders, I vote for anyone but me. Rejection stings a bit, and I'm getting a sense that I won't be getting many votes."

Seraph impulsively went to raise his hand. Who but him was better suited to lead? After all, he had the most experience in the dungeon and with working with dungeon teams? While that may be true, it was not experience he could pull from to gather support for himself just yet. At least, not until he was certain that enough of a gap existed that others wouldn't pose a danger to him. He quickly banished the thought, chastising himself, and lowered his hand as quickly as he had raised it.

Paul raised his hand. "It might not be what you guys are looking for, but I did a little time in the service. Six years active and another two years on drilling status. If anyone objects, it doesn't hurt my feelings to pass it up," Paul said, looking at Alexander.

"Man, don't give me that look," Alexander said. "I just don't know you guys. I'm tired, I'm annoyed, and I'm irritated, and I just don't think it's okay to be prying at each other's secrets right now. I'm not out to be a dick or anything, it just is what it is. If you want to be in charge, that's fine by me. You've got my vote. Happy?

"Also, just in case anyone needed to know, the bathrooms are there and there." Alexander pointed to the farthest corners of the gymnasium—the right side and then the left. "You're welcome, guys. Boys room on the right, and girls on the left."

"Um, guys. If you've got to go, go now," Erin said, pointing upwards. The pregame clock had turned on, and the timer had been set to ten minutes.

"Alright, guys, you heard her. We're not taking any risks here, though. Battle buddy teams. Sorry, but if you've got to go, take a friend. Erin, if you have to go take Luca," Paul said. "Here's the chain of command. If anything happens to me, Jack takes over, and if anything happens to him, Alexander takes over, then Erin, and after that... well, Luca, just try to make it out of here. Alright, everyone, go. You've got five minutes and then it's back here with weapons out."

"And... break," interjected Jack, but nobody seemed amused.

Event Notice: When the countdown stops, you must successfully defend yourself from a horde of monsters.

Reward: Access to the rest of the school.

Conditional Reward: +1 to all stats for the person who kills the most monsters.

"Stop!" yelled Paul. "Everyone, back here. Something is happening."

Just as quickly as everyone was prepared to run away for a quick break, they stopped and retreated back toward one another, circling up as the lights went completely dark. A projector screen came down from the rafters, and a colored video flashed across the room and onto the screen. A cartoonish bard-looking man walked across the screen and looked down at the group. It was the same cartoon figure they had seen before during orientation.

"Great. This is perfect. You are all still here, at least. Well, those of you who made it this far. Phase II is going to start very, very soon. Now, when that timer hits zero, the doors to this gym are going to unlock, and let me warn you right now, there are some pretty scary and serious things on the other side of that door. But to move on and away from here means finding tokens that have been hidden throughout the area on the other side of that door. Be careful though, because the rest of the school is full of monsters—except for the office. That's the designated safe zone if you need to rest. Remember now, you need ten tokens to leave the area and proceed to Phase III. Good luck to you all, and do try to stay alive."

The projection ended, and the screen rolled back up as the lights turned on.

Notification: Quest Granted – Each member of the party must collect 10 tokens to advance to the final phase.

Reward: Transition into the Third Phase. 30 Experience, 10 Sol.

"Alright. Looks like we've got no time to work out any sort of strategy," said Paul, a hint of concern on his face as the gym door started to bulge forward as if pushed by a giant force on the other side.

Seraph knew a bit more about survival in the dungeon. He knew that standing out in the open like this was a poor idea. He didn't want to die either, and poor preparation was an easy way to meet a messy end. "We should retreat to the bathroom. It should be a smaller space, so we can defend it easier and not get swarmed by any monsters that show up. It'll let us set up a kill point that everyone can go back and forth from to even out any experience gains."

Paul nodded, examining Seraph and feeling that there was something more to the answers and his son's sudden insights, but he couldn't quite put it into words. He hesitated. "OK, hold what you got. Everybody, run to the men's bathroom. Let's go get in front of this thing."

CHAPTER 8:
BETRAYAL

The five of them ran straight into the men's bathroom. The sound of their shoes squeaking as they ran across the court mixed with the constant pounding echoes coming from the entryway. Alexander struggled to keep up the pace that the others set and lagged behind them. The clock shone brightly in red as the numbers ticked down, getting ever closer to zero.

As they all ran, their focus was forward on their goal of escaping the pending danger. Afraid to see what they would find if they looked. Afraid to see what they were running from—except for Seraph. He saw that he was the only one who wasn't afraid, noticing that with each booming blow against the door, the plaster surrounding the metal door frame fell off in pieces. The closer to zero the clock got, the bigger the pieces were that fell.

As they all passed through the swinging doorway into the bathroom, Seraph instantly regretted the decision to direct the group to seek shelter inside it when he realized how small the area was. Things would be cramped, and he was not the only one to come to that conclusion. He noticed the turned heads and glares coming his way from Alexander and Jack, while Erin was unwilling to look at him, and his father had other concerns on his mind. It was clear to him that the group regretted their decision to listen to his advice.

"So, what's the plan here, champ?" questioned Jack, an obvious edge to his voice.

Seraph wasn't sure what the plan would be. This was a bathroom connected to a basketball court in a gymnasium. He had assumed the bathroom would either be bigger, or it would connect to an adjacent locker room. Instead, he was looking at the same thing everyone else was. Two porcelain sinks and a cracked mirror between them, a dual urinal against the wall, a lone bathroom stall, and a locker full of sports equipment with a padlock on it.

"I don't know," Seraph admitted, returning the glares with a glare of his own. "I thought there would be a locker room back here, and we would then be able to build up some quick defenses and work on kiting whatever is coming our way. I thought we could use the environment to our advantage, but I don't see how we can do that now."

Paul caught the frustration in his son's voice. He had no intention of letting anyone in the group die, and on some level, Seraph knew that. The danger was not unbeatable. Seraph was angry with himself for making a decision that ended up being wrong. Though he knew that a tutorial wasn't a place for a party wipe, it didn't change the fact that the group was about to have a very difficult time in the name of growth.

"That's why there's a chain of command, kiddo," said Paul. "Let this be a good learning experience. You undercut my authority after the group agreed to let me lead them to safety and made the decision that led us here. It's not on you, though. This is on me. I let it happen, and as group leader that falls on me."

"Don't worry, everyone. I've got a plan to get us all out of here. I promise," Paul said as he addressed the group. Truthfully, he didn't have a plan yet, but as the leader, it fell on him to make sure morale didn't completely dissipate. But before he could say anything else or give any kind of pep talk to boost morale and get people ready to fight, a loud crash could be heard from the gymnasium.

They had run out of time.

Switching gears and switching roles, Paul turned to yell at the group. "Weapons out!" he ordered as he pulled his own long knife from a sheath on his leg and overturned the sports locker on its side to provide some cover.

Seraph matched the action by pulling his mace from his belt loop. Seraph had to admit, his father cut quite the intimidating figure. Something about the way he carried himself and the aura he cast let others know this man had been a killer. Something Seraph recognized and respected.

Alexander was the next to willingly come forward bearing his weapon, surprising Paul and Seraph when he pulled a short metal rod from his pocket and pressed a switch that caused the rod to extend, ending on a point. "Pocket spear," he explained, shrugging sheepishly. "I don't really know how to use it, but I figure I can just jab a lot. It's better than sitting around and crying, hoping that somebody is going to save me."

Paul nodded in approval but inwardly groaned, reminded of the fact that these guys were all rookies. "Sure, that'll work. Just try to be careful you don't stab any of us. Most of you are new to holding a weapon, so try to be careful. No flashy movements or power moves. This isn't television, and you'll just hurt yourself or someone else."

He then looked at the other two, his expression changing to one of hardened anger. "Well, what's the problem, you two? Where are your weapons?"

Erin looked downward, unable to meet his gaze as she wrapped her fingers around each other in a show of anxiety. "I've got a claw. I think I wear it like a baseball glove, but I don't feel comfortable getting that close up. I'm not a fighter, and I'm not strong like the rest of you."

Seraph looked at her arm down toward her wrist where a leather strap wrapped around her forearm that ended in multiple blades. A Cat's Claw he guessed. It was a weapon he was more used to. Far more used to than the mace in his hand, in fact. If she wasn't going to defend herself, he had no issues with taking it from her later.

"Fine," said Paul, unable to hide the frustration in his voice. "You can stay with my son toward the back. Just make sure you keep him safe. And as for you," he said as he pointed a finger at Jack, "where's your weapon?"

"Yeah, about that. I don't actually have one," answered Jack. "They gave me a defensive piece instead of a weapon," he explained as he opened his shirt to show dark chain mail with razor edges. "Basically, anything that attacks me, is going to get hurt too. It'll help shield me from harm. Your kid can hide behind me too, it's fine."

Paul glared, furious at the level of cowardice he was seeing between these two, but whatever score he was keeping, this was not the time to settle it.

Seraph tried not to be too obvious by rolling his eyes. While technically correct, thornmail did reflect damage back on the attacker, but this wasn't thornmail, it was razormail—a weapon of the melee fighter, and a way to inflict additional damage as bodies crashed into each other and maneuvered in close combat. This was no shield; it was a weapon.

"Alright, new plan," said Paul, "because wearing razor blades isn't going to help us right now. So, Jack, listen up. I'm counting on you. You and Erin will be in the back with Luca. Protect him. If anything happens to him, you'll have to answer to me. I'll be up front, taking the brunt of the attack, and Alexander will be supporting me as much as he can from the rear with the reach of his spear.

Paul continued shifting his gaze. "Alexander, if there's something I can't kill, I'll be pitching it back to you to pin down with your spear. Hopefully, the lot of you can finish off whatever I don't kill."

Paul turned to the other man with his hand pointed like a knife. "And, Jack, just milling around in the back isn't going to cut it. You can grab that mop over there and snap it in two. It might not be much, but it's better than just sitting on your hands, and you'll at least have something to stab them with."

Seraph couldn't fault the plan on such short notice, but he had no intention of waiting safely in the back. The dungeon by nature punished those who avoided growth and rewarded those who dared. That was the mark of the warrior—the willingness to engage the enemy—and Seraph was willing. He would not allow himself to fall behind due to the well-meaning actions of his father, who didn't seem to realize that the action he suggested would do nothing but endanger him, if his growth did not keep up with the demands of the dungeon.

It was a mistake Seraph had seen many families make before as he recalled a memory of the screaming families he had separated when he had chosen those he thought would survive in the dungeon, leaving or killing the rest.

A loud scream reverberated through the gym as a monster flew through the air and landed with a sickening wet thud on the ground directly in front of them. As blood began to spread and pool from the splattered corpse, the moment of truth was at hand.

"Oh my god, oh my god, oh my god!" screamed Erin as she pressed her body against the far wall of the bathroom, curling up. "This can't be happening. I make coffee for a living; I can't do this. I'm sorry. I'm so sorry." She started sobbing, throwing her weapon off as she ran into the stall and locked it behind her. They would have to figure that one out later.

Paul gave her a look of contempt—a look Seraph appreciated that his father could give. He quickly banished the look as his father's face was replaced with an expression of grim worry. Whatever he was going to say to her was quickly cut short as the sound of monsters fighting each other to fit through the gymnasium doorway echoed and filled the air.

His father grasped his knife and motioned with his hands for the rest of them to hunker down and be quiet. Seraph ignored it as he pushed forward to look at the swarm of monsters as his father tried to grab him and haul him back. He needed to know what came through that door. All their lives might depend on it. What he saw brought him some relief. Short and furry Kobolds, their faces long with a rat-like face on skinny pale bodies, covered in short, matted fur slick with grease and grime. They walked hunched over on two legs, with long arms that end in clawed hands featuring three fingers. Basic fodder.

Seraph counted twenty-two of the rat-faced monsters, but they were not the primary threat that stood between them and continuing onward. It was the Gigas that stood at the splintered doorway. A giant man-monster, it stood twice as tall as a regular person, weighing at least hundreds of pounds—all of which were thick, corded muscle. Though it appeared slow, the monster was deadly. The force of its blows were the same as being struck by a moving vehicle, and its fists were devastating. It was a monster that Seraph, with all his experience, did not believe they could defeat. They were without a measure of luck, and the use of skills that Seraph did not believe the group possessed.

He felt hands on his shoulders pulling him back into the relative safety of the bathroom.

He turned and looked to see Paul and Alexander looking at him like he was crazy. "What are you doing?" asked Paul. "You could have been killed. What part of listen do you not understand? You need to stay behind me where I know you're safe." From behind them, Jack tried to hide a grin as he snickered.

Seraph looked at his father, his own face just as grim, and he hesitated to do or say more. He had not wanted to expose himself more than he already had, but he felt he had little choice.

"I needed to know what was coming at us, so I could advise you. Those things on the other side of this wall, they're called Kobolds. They're nothing. They're trash, and we won't have a problem killing all of them, but that monster that leads them, it's a Gigas. That's something that's going to be hard to kill. If we get trapped in here and it connects an attack, it'll likely kill all of us. It's going to be difficult to hurt it too. It has a tough outer skin that's hard to penetrate."

Paul looked at him suspiciously, as did the other two men. "Just how exactly do you know this, Luca?"

In another life, Seraph knew of an old saying that could be applied here. In the absence of a good lie, tell the truth—or at least parts of it. "We don't have time for that now, but I promise I'll tell you everything when we do."

Paul put his hands on his wrist, and Seraph's eyes lit up in anger as Paul raised his voice, "No, I don't think I will. Tell me now. Tell me why I should trust you on this."

Seraph responded, "I have the Restart ability. It's a super-rare ability, so I'm discouraged from mentioning it without good justification. I've already used it a few times. When I die, I go back in time to certain points in my adventures. This is one of them. I've already been through this battle before. Though I can only go back to a set point once."

Paul seemed to contemplate the viability of the answer, and he simply nodded. He would go for it, for now, as would the other men. They might not believe him, but they had few reasons to doubt that what he said was true.

The look Paul gave Seraph let him know that he had his doubts. He had clearly noticed a few contradictions and things that didn't make sense. But this was not the time to figure out the reason for half-truths and lies.

"Guys! Hey, guys! This has been a nice little chit-chat you all are having, it really is, but they're here!" screamed Jack as the first group of Kobolds approached, crossing the threshold and leading away from the gymnasium and into the bathroom where they were hidden.

Paul gripped his knife tightly as they all braced themselves. Erin stumbled out of the stall sobbing and went to hide beneath the sinks as she rocked back-and-forth, unable to aid the party as she quaked with fear and shame.

Eyes moving, Seraph watched as Alexander took up position behind Paul. Something was up with Jack, though. Seraph could tell by the way he was shifting his eyes. He was a man looking for a way out. Like a rabbit looking for a chance to run. The weak always had such a look. Seraph moved to back up Alexander, his father making a wordless protest that died in his throat as he realized the safest place for his son was right beside him. Even if it was fighting at his side.

As the first of the Kobolds ran into the lockers that Paul had pushed over, their movement halted. Their numbers could not easily navigate the wedge that had been created with the bulwark and the entryway. The group couldn't help but smile as the monsters spoke in their strange language, appearing to curse each other as they tripped up each other's movements. Animals.

Seraph knew that they would make short work of the Kobolds. It was never a question to him. Though the Kobolds were monsters, they were weak, unarmed, and unarmored. The only real danger they posed were their numbers, and their tails could be swung to try to knock a person off balance. None of which mattered as they funneled together, unable to use the very things that made them dangerous. The idea to seek refuge in the bathroom had paid off after all.

The first Kobold tried to bridge the gap by forcing its way through the bulwark, its jaws salivating in hunger as its clawed hand reached over the overturned lockers. As it tried to pull itself over to get to the other side, Paul thrust his knife forward and upwards with deadly purpose. The knife cut through flesh and lodged into the creature's eye, killing it instantly, but was lodged in the fleshy membrane of the monster's eyeball. As the body fell, the knife fell with it.

Alexander worked to cover the gap as Paul struggled to dislodge his knife. Unlike Paul, Alexander wasn't looking for kills as he thrust his spear out, again and again, looking to stab and injure the mass of Kobolds in front of him. His were not measured hits, but rather desperate attacks. As much as he could, Alexander used his strength to lift and throw some of the monsters back for Jack and Seraph to kill.

Paul realized he had over committed in his

own attack as he watched Alexander struggle but somehow single-handily keep the pressing monsters at bay. Paul vowed to not over-commit again as the knife finally came free, giving a discreet nod of thanks to Alexander for keeping the rat-faced monsters off him. Alexander shot him a thumbs-up, and the movement was enough to distract both of them as one of the Kobolds was able to push their defenses, slashing with its claws at Paul's face. Its fangs aimed for the neck, only to be met by a premature end as Seraph's mace crashed down on its skull, caving in a side of its face. It fell lifelessly to the ground with an almost shocked look on its face.

A metallic clang hit the ground where the Kobold had fallen, and Seraph saw a bronze token —much like what could be found in an arcade —had fallen to the ground. He noted it, but he couldn't safely collect it yet.

Both men turned to look at Seraph, surprised that he had been able to intervene like that. Seraph yelled at the two. "Pull yourself out of it. There's still a bunch of these things we've got to kill. Just try to police up as many of the tokens as you can. They're going to be our ticket out of here."

The three worked in symmetry as the other two members of their party largely remained uninvolved, Jack occasionally hitting the Kobolds he was able to get free hits on, and Erin had at least quit sobbing.

They continued their grim work until all the Kobolds were dead, their bodies scattered around the floor slick with blood. Their own bodies were covered in filth and sweat, a deep fatigue setting into their bones, and of the Gigas, there was not a word or sound. As Seraph peeked out and saw it, he found it still right at the doorway leading out of the Gymnasium, up into the rest of the school.

As the last Kobold died, a series of prompts flashed before each of them, awarding individual experience for their participation, and prompting level-ups and quest updates. Seraph ignored the level up prompts; he would have to allot his points later when he had a free moment to better map out a build path.

Notification: The Event has successfully concluded. All party members may now freely leave the gymnasium to explore the rest of the school.

Party Member - JACK - has earned the conditional award of +1 to all stats.

They all looked at him, angrily wondering how he had managed to cheat his way to the reward when he had just sat back and let the rest of them do the work. He smiled back, knowing the reason behind their anger. "Sorry. Sorry, guys. It's just that I wanted to make sure those monsters were dead, and so I went around when you were all busy and made sure that they wouldn't be getting out. Basically, double-tap, right? Just doing my job. I'm sorry it worked out like this."

They were all angry with him, and Alexander stepped toward him, grabbing his shirt and pulling him closer, yelling, "You didn't deserve to win that; you didn't do anything. You cheated."

With his newly changed strength, Jack easily removed Alexander's hands, his smile replaced by a look of cruel disregard. "Oh, I did plenty. I used the resources I had, and already I'm the strongest person here. But I feel bad for this I really do; I am sorry, for what it's worth."

"You sure don't seem sorry," Paul accused as he stepped toward Jack, his fists clenched ready to attack the man. "Otherwise you wouldn't be gloating about how you cheated me and Alexander out of that reward."

"Oh, you're right," responded Jack fearfully as he backed away from Paul. "I'm not sorry about that. I'm sorry about this," he said as he held up a handful of tokens, and as quick as Seraph was able to realize there were ten tokens in his hands, he was gone.

Notification: With the loss of a party member, you currently have 3 tokens. You require 37 more tokens for the entire party to advance.

CHAPTER 9: DISCOVERY

Seraph felt a blind fury he hadn't felt in an age, and from the looks of anger on the faces of the rest of the group, he knew he wasn't alone. It was one thing to be a freeloader and get carried by the group—a freeloader at least wants to grow stronger. It was another thing entirely to steal the drops.

If there was anything Seraph hated more than the weak it was a thief, and a thief had stolen something precious to him—a ticket out of the second phase of the tutorial. Seraph clenched his hand into a fist, imagining tearing the man's soul from his body, malleable like crimson clay in his hands, destroying piece by piece his immortal being as a consequence for the theft. Seraph made a solemn promise to himself and to the dungeon that Jack would be a victim of his wrath.

> Notification: An ability of the Black Seraph has been unsealed. Condition met - Make a binding oath while influenced by an emotional impulse.

> Notification: Passive Unlocked - The Dark Heart - Aspect of Wrath - When enacting vengeance or retribution, the user's strength and agility are doubled.

Dark magic began to flow through his veins, showing through his skin like black spiderwebs, and an ominous tense aura began to pulse out from his core in waves. While the others might not have known what was happening to him, they all knew that something had changed, and that Jack's betrayal was the likely catalyst.

A hand clapped down on his shoulder, calming him. Having calmed down, his new passive buff deactivated, and with it the forbidding aura that had been circulating around him dissipated.

"Alright, so that sucked. Like that was completely terrible," Paul lamented, trying to salvage the mood as he saw the dark expressions of anger on their faces. "But I think we've all learned a valuable lesson here about leaving our valuables out." He was trying to make a joke to lighten the mood, but it wasn't well-received as neither Alexander nor Seraph smiled at it. He still counted it as a win though, because the dark tense air around them suddenly dispersed, and Erin gave him a small smile from beneath her hiding place.

At least, he had their attention. As a leader, and as a father, it fell on him to try to keep the group morale up, and even if they were obviously unhappy, so long as he had their attention, he could work on that. "See, you guys, I actually learned a very valuable lesson. Did you know you heal after a battle? I was pretty sure I had at least one stab wound and a few pretty big cuts, scrapes, and bruises, and it's only been a few minutes since the fighting stopped, but it's all gone now. That's pretty amazing. Which is a good thing too since that big thing over there looks like he's going to be a handful," Paul explained.

"I'll have to take your word on it, I wouldn't know," Alexander said, slyly perking up and joining the conversation. "But you know, Paul, unlike you with your stab-stab action with that oversized knife, the whole point of a spear is to keep a little distance so as to not have to worry about having something you need to recover from after."

It was a good point, thought Seraph, and some good-natured ribbing did help people to bond. In the dungeon, having those kinds of bonds with others could be the difference between life and death.

Even he had, in his other life, counted on those bonds. He had counted on his comrades. He dismissed the thoughts from his head. He didn't need to indulge in memories of friends from his other life. The present was what mattered, and if he did things right, he would see them again. At least it was good that the others were seeing the miraculous healing of the dungeon for themselves. Some things were just easier when seen rather than explained.

"Oh my god. I'm so sorry." They all turned and looked at the woman who had formerly been sobbing underneath the sink. "I just don't know what came over me. It's like I lost my mind for a minute; I just couldn't control myself," Erin explained as she tried to smooth out the track marks of bleeding mascara on her face. Paul and Alexander looked at each other and rolled their eyes.

"It's alright," replied Seraph. "This is a learning point too. What you experienced was a status effect called fear. It has a small chance of afflicting a person anytime their hidden courage stat falls below a certain threshold. It does happen, and just like people's bodies heal after a battle, so too does the mind. Just try to do better in the future." Seraph didn't care if she lived or died long-term, he just needed her to stay alive long enough to use her ability—and harvest that same ability from her if she proved in the future to continue to be incapable.

Seraph turned to look at his father. "Alright, so what's the plan, Dad? We still need to find more of these tokens, and from the look of it, we're going to have to kill more monsters for that to happen."

Paul let the question linger for a minute, going over it in his head before looking back at Seraph with an eyebrow raised. "Oh, you want to ask me what the plan is? Why ask me anything when it's clear that you're the one with all the answers. Why don't you just be the leader? It's not like you listened to me anyway."

This was something Seraph had been afraid of happening. There was an edge to Paul's voice. Things were changing between them at a rapid rate, both from the exposure to the dungeon and their shared experience so far in it. Seraph had revealed too much, and it was more than the man's processing could handle. "It's not like that, I told you. I have a restart ability, and for that reason, I had some foreknowledge because of my ability that you didn't have. I didn't want anyone to die. This wasn't my first time fighting this battle." Seraph lied with ease, hoping to not have to continue the subject before holes in his arguments were discovered.

This was not something he wanted to be debating. This was the problem with humans, and regular humans at that. They insisted on wasting time at the wrong moments, debating the obvious when it was neither the time nor place to do so. Reckless. His plan, while not perfect, had ended up okay. No one was hurt, and no one died.

Paul gave him a harsh glare, his eyes narrowed in hostility, and his body tensed with frustration. "Oh, still going on about that restart ability I see. Don't you think it's getting a little tired? We all know you didn't restart or respawn or whatever you want to call it. Well, I'm on to you since you don't want to come clean."

"Here's one," Paul explained, pointing toward the exit. "You said that thing over there, the Gigas, it's something we can't kill. You said we need to get out of here before it comes after and kills us. That's what you said, right? Well, it hasn't moved a bit—except to stay near the door. That's one lie I've caught you in already. Besides, if my decades of gaming experience have taught me anything, it's that either it's on a proxy defend of the entry point and will only attack if we get close, or its optional content."

It was decent thinking Seraph mused, *and it wasn't wrong.* At least, about Seraph lying. The verdict was still out regarding the Gigas, but Paul was likely right, though it had been an educated guess when he had made his claims. The fact that Paul wasn't wrong didn't make it easier on him to defuse the situation, though he suspected that anything he said at this point would be the wrong thing to say. Having no options, he chose to say nothing in response.

Alexander pushed forward, wanting in on the conversation, interested, and demanding to be more involved in the discussion. Meanwhile, Erin moved farther away, staying in the back, and thankful that the spotlight wasn't on her. "What are you getting at, Paul? I thought this was your kid."

Paul shrugged. "I did too. But a lot is changing pretty quickly, and things aren't adding up to me. But here's what I'm going to do. I'm going to kill that thing. Maybe we can sneak past it, and maybe it won't even attack us if we try to just walk by it, but I don't think so. What I do know from all of my gaming experience, is that these tutorials never introduce a boss too difficult to beat. That would ruin the fun. From my work experience, I know no company wants the onboarding to be too difficult. Otherwise, they lose too much if somebody can't hack it. So that thing over there might be terrible, but I don't believe we can't manage to take it down. We just need to figure out the best way to approach it. But if I'm going to kill it, I'm going to need you guys to help and back me up."

Seraph looked at him. He kept his face stoic and unresponsive, not wanting to influence the man's decision, or the decision of the group. If they made the decision to try to kill it, he wouldn't get in the way of that. This was how people got stronger, by challenging the impossible and pushing their limits. As it used to be said: impossible is nothing.

In the end, Seraph decided to speak up. "If you're serious about this, I'll help as much as I can, but I can't promise I'll be able to save anyone if that thing ends up being too strong for our group. I know you three don't know what you're getting yourself into, but try to be careful here. We don't know what lies ahead beyond the Gigas."

Paul's eyes narrowed in annoyance as he hardened his heart and made a decision. "It's not your place to second guess me. I don't need you to save me, and I don't need you to look out for me. I don't know you, not really. It's been bothering me, but you're not my son, and I'm going to figure out a way to get him back. Back from you. Whoever you are."

For all of his anger and accusation, Seraph knew that Paul wasn't wrong, though it was complicated. It was not something Seraph took personally. When he looked at Paul, he didn't see an angry man, he saw a defeated man venting frustration, and his main frustration wasn't wrong. His world had changed in fundamental ways, and Seraph wasn't his son—at least, the same son he had this morning. "Do what you need to do," Seraph said. "But, as for me, my eyes are on the door. I'll help if I can, but I won't die for this."

Paul ran his fingers through his hair, showing his increasing anxiety, anger, and embarrassment. Unsure of what to say.

It was Erin who intervened. "Look, let's all take a step back and just wait a minute, alright, before anyone does anything they might regret. Things are a little heated right now, so instead of antagonizing each other, let's let things simmer down and settle before re-engaging. I'm sure everyone needs to adjust themselves and work around with their stats?"

Paul nodded his head in agreement. "You're right. I need to assign my stats. I'm level 5 now, and it looks like I get two points per level, so I've ten stat points to spend. I'm thinking of going all-in on strength."

"So, what are you leaning toward?" asked Alexander. "I leveled up too. I'm level 3 now, and I'm extremely unfamiliar with how to build. I'm open to ideas, though."

They both looked at Seraph. "Well, Luca, do you have any insight into this level up business?" asked Alexander with a grin. "You know, on account of you being an expert? I mean, you've done this before right…"

Erin shifted uncomfortably as Alexander and Paul both looked at Seraph with questioning eyes.

"Yeah, I do. I have some insight into the matter," replied Seraph, coldly looking Alexander right in the eye, and thinking that he had chosen the wrong person to target with his wrath. "Whatever you do, don't try to min-max your stat selections. These aren't arbitrary numbers. It's your body. You need to understand that you have to upgrade your stats relative to each other. If you upgrade your strength too much, but not your endurance, you'll break your own bones every time you move. If you forget to upgrade your perception, you'll find yourself easily breaking doors, drinking glasses, the floor, you name it, all because you'll be lacking the ability to regulate yourself."

"Wow, seriously? I didn't know that could happen," replied Alexander, his mind blown as he realized what he was going to do with his stats would have completely backfired. "Thanks for telling me that. It's a real lifesaver."

"I wasn't finished," chided Seraph. "It works the same way with agility and perception. Have you ever waved your hand in front of your face and seen only a blur? Well, if you upgrade your agility without keeping pace with your perception, all your senses do that same thing, and then it doesn't matter how fast you are because your perception of your own speed can't keep up with your ability to process it."

All three of them were fixated on what he had to say. "What about luck and intelligence? What do those do?"

Seraph sighed. He hated having to bluntly interpret data for those who couldn't infer the answers from the existing pool of knowledge they had. "Intelligence governs how many skills you can hold and how fast some of the skills progress. But likewise, you don't want to ignore it either. There are going to be times that you need to be quick on your feet and think of solutions to problems—quicker than anything you've experienced. As for luck. Well, luck just affects your loot pulls from the loot table, nothing else."

Paul looked at him in embarrassment and asked the question on his mind. "Are you really my son? Are you my Luca?"

Seraph looked at him, contemplating how best to answer. There was no other way around the truth, so Seraph would give him a version of it that the man could tolerate. "Yes, I am your son. But I'm not Luca, not really. I haven't gone by that name in a long time. I spent over thirty years in this dungeon before dying and triggering my restart ability. When I died, I bled to death at the end of a massive battle. I was a little older than you are now."

"Holy...wow, just wow," Alexander said as Erin looked on with something like pity. She touched Paul's shoulder to comfort him as the man's eyes looked to the ground as he processed the admission. For a brief moment, a few tears dropped from his face, but as quickly as they came, they were gone.

With his eyes red but having regained his composure, he looked toward Seraph and asked, "So, what do we do now?"

Seraph replied, "We continue what we're doing. We survive, we grow, and I do what I can to keep you guys alive. Oh, and you stay the team leader."

Paul scoffed. "Why? Why should I stay the team leader when you can clearly do this so much better than me?"

Seraph smiled a rare smile as he tried to fix the situation. "No, I can't. I basically ran solo. I had teams I worked with, but I wasn't on a team myself. This is something you can do, and something you can teach me. We can work with that. From now on, call me Seraph. It's been my name a long time now."

"Because of those wings on the emblem you got? The wings I made fun of you for?" asked

Paul.

"Yeah," answered Seraph. "I was given back my legendary class when I restarted. I didn't think it would be the case. I thought I'd have to work my way up again. In one sense, you could think of it as a new game plus mode. It just hasn't been unlocked yet for me to use it."

"Well, I guess I can see why Paul might be ready to believe you—or at least not doubt you since you're related and all. But why should me and Erin believe anything you say?" asked Alexander.

"Because my dad isn't wrong. The Gigas can be killed, and since I don't need to hide what I know anymore, I'm going to tell you how we can kill it. All of us are going to take it out. But first, we are going to fix up your stats. Dad put 5 points into strength, 3 points into agility, and 2 points into perception. Alexander, your call what you do, but until you can learn some finesse and find some training, you should focus on your endurance. Erin, I'm not sure if you got any points, but if you get any, put them all into intelligence. It'll also help to prevent you from suffering from mental-based status effects.

"What about you?" asked Paul. "What are you building toward?"

Seraph thought for a second. He hadn't actually considered what he was building toward.

"Honestly, I haven't thought about it," he admitted. "It's been full-on, ever since I woke up in this body, and before committing to any plan of action, I'd like to do some analysis on what I could have done differently build-wise. But for now, I only hit level 3, so I don't feel bad assigning the stats I'm working with. With these 6 points, I'll be splitting them evenly between agility and perception for now. Erin, I know I told you to spend all your points on intelligence, but it might be better if you split them between intelligence and endurance. It will help keep the fear effect from triggering again, and if it does trigger, it won't last as long, that will at least offer some resistance to it. We need to be prepared for what is to come. Now, who's ready to kill a Gigas?"

Everyone raised their hand, and for a minute, Seraph thought this might have been a good idea.

CHAPTER 10: TEAMWORK

To everyone's surprise, Erin jumped at the opportunity to step forward and lead the way. According to Seraph's plan, she didn't need to do much. She just needed to be the first one out, so she could use her ability and then maintain the ability in a pending state as the rest of their group did their own parts, waiting for the signal to release it.

"Alright, guys. On the count of three, everyone needs to go. Remember your roles, stick to the plan, and you'll be just fine," Seraph said as he looked at each of them, waiting until he got a nod in affirmation that they understood what their role was in the takedown of the Gigas. One after another they gave him the acknowledgment he was looking for.

Satisfied, he began the countdown. "One, two, three, go," Seraph commanded in a low voice.

They ran out into the exposed danger of the gymnasium from their hiding place, each of them shielding their eyes as Erin pulled upon the innate power of her passive ability, Starcall. A white light barely the size of a tennis ball blinked into existence at the feet of the giant monster, though the monster seemed not to notice as it stood passive and unmoving near the exit. The light blinked and pulsed, but if the Gigas noticed, it refused to look, completely unconcerned about the thing at its feet.

Alexander was the first to strike. He ran up the wooden bleachers to give himself a chance to strike at the unprotected side of the Gigas. With the noise in the room as loud as it was, his footsteps landing heavy on the steps as he ran up them did nothing to alert the monster that he was coming. The monster's attention focused completely on Seraph as he ran toward it.

The elven man pulled his spear from his pocket—extending it as he leveled it—and charged, bracing the spear with his body and shoving it into the side of the Gigas, who screamed in rage as it counter-attacked and brought a fist down, breaking the bleachers where Alexander had seconds previously been standing. The attack only missing due to Seraph's instructions to move backward immediately after striking, having informed the group of the Gigas' attack patterns.

The monster, seeing Alexander still alive, bellowed in rage. The scream threw everyone into a short state of fear. A fear that stopped Alexander where he was in paralysis as the Gigas gave chase. Its attention fixated on him with a terrible look. Eyes of the deepest gray bore straight into him, full of pain and anger. They all knew that if Alexander got caught, the thing would be merciless and take its time relishing killing him.

"Uh, guys, I got its attention!" Alexander yelled, his voice cracking as it betrayed his fear as he tried to pretend to be more confident than he really was. "I need help, though. I can't move. I'm stuck. I can't move at all, guys. I'm really stuck."

"I have you, Alexander. Just breathe and be ready to move when you get the signal," Seraph replied as he ran behind the Gigas into the monster's blind spot. He tightly gripped the mace in his hand and aimed his strike at the back of the monster's ankle, bringing all of his strength against it, hoping the effort would shatter the bone and cripple it.

The Gigas roared in anger as it quickly turned its hulking body, its arms swinging out in all directions to catch and kill the man that had tried to harm it. "Alexander, that's the signal! You need to move, move, move!" yelled Seraph as he worked to dodge the blows that were coming his way. Every strike the Gigas threw was devastating. If even one of those punches landed, Seraph knew it would kill him in a gory end.

"I wasn't able to cripple it like we planned. It's still mobile! Careful, guys!" Seraph shouted, giving everyone else a clear warning.

Alexander ran out of the way, jumping around the bleachers, barely staying ahead of the monster. As Alexander moved, the Gigas followed. Its oversized fists caught on pieces of the bleachers, tearing off boards and planks with a glancing touch, the remaining parts pulverized instantly into dust. When Alexander finally realized the Gigas was no longer following him, he panted, out of breath, sweat rolling off his body as he looked at the path of destruction that had followed him.

"Get back into position, Alexander! While I've got his attention, just be ready to go again!" yelled Seraph. Alexander swallowed hard and forced himself to push his fears down as deep as they would go as he tried to find a foothold on the broken wooden planks. He needed to maneuver himself back toward the Gigas and the weak point that Seraph had exposed by holding its attention—the back of the neck. One step after another, running as fast as he could over the broken patching, he shot forward, thrusting his spear with all the force he could use, and he jammed the spear into the monster's neck. But it was not enough; the thing was barely harmed. A thin line of blood was the full extent of the damage he had caused the monster.

This time, the Gigas screamed as it brought both of its fists down as Alexander scrambled to get out of the way. Both Seraph and Alexander immediately realized he wasn't going to be able to run to safety.

"Just jump!" Seraph shouted as loudly as he could.

Alexander heard it and jumped off the bleachers, just as the Gigas' fists crashed down, destroying the remaining portions of the bleachers that Alexander had been just been standing on. The Gigas, not to be deterred, picked up a piece of the shattered boards and went to throw it at the man.

Seraph, hesitated for a moment wondering if maybe he should let the Gigas kill Alexander to get a larger share of the loot before dismissing it and moving in to attack. Though he had been unsuccessful in his first attempt to try to cripple the giant—the bones too dense and sturdy for Seraph to damage at his current level —he believed he could still damage the creature if he shifted the focus of his attack, and in doing so, he might be able to save Alexander.

He needed to focus on a different target— something weaker than the bones of the ankle had been. He quickly realized the top of the monster's foot was likely what he was looking for. It should be less protected and less durable. With time running out, it would have to do.

Gripping his weapon in his hand, he manipulated his thoughts to boost his strength, focusing on his anger—and the targets of his anger —to activate the Dark Heart - Aspect of Wrath ability. As new power flooded into his veins, he knew he had succeeded.

With a yell, he smashed his mace against the top of the Gigas' foot. A snap could be heard as the tiny bones just beneath the surface broke against the pressure of the blow. As the bones broke, and the soft tissue was destroyed from the impact, the Gigas dropped the board it had been getting ready to throw.

Now was the moment of truth. The monster howled in extreme pain—each scream drastically improving its reflexes and exponentially increasing the danger it posed to the group—and though Seraph had been prepared for the pain, he was still caught by the force of the vibrations as the monster smashed its fists into the ground, causing the floor to cascade like a wave.

Seraph landed sprawled out on the ground near Alexander. Though he had dodged the bulk of the blow, he was unable to completely evade the damage the monster caused. With no further plan to play, Seraph shouted, "Now!" hoping the situation with the balls figured out.

Erin saw Seraph fall and knew that to be the first signal. Seraph had explained that once the monster was fully immersed in chasing down one of them, she would need to release her ability, and she did so as a blinding light filled the room as monster glaring down at him as it moved in to finish the kill, just as Seraph called out, "Now!"

They all shielded their eyes to not be blinded by the effects of her ability. It didn't do any damage; it just inflicted a status effect—an effect that even worked on bosses, as long as they looked in the direction of the Starcall spawn. It was an effect that had clearly taken hold as the monster clutched at its eye, unable to see as it roared in anger and confusion as it flailed its arms about.

This is what they had wanted. A single moment of vulnerability as it screamed to the sky, its anger heavy in the room as Seraph ran over to Alexander and dragged him out of its way. Just in time, as it began to rampage indiscriminately. Paul jumped from the rafters, knife in hand, and performed a swan dive, directly into the eye of the rampaging Gigas. He had used his ability to reach the rafters of the gymnasium—the highest point that he could reach—and then did as he had been instructed: wait for the right moment, wait for the signal, and then unleash himself on the monster.

Paul threw his body like a spear, and the knife he carried on his person was the tip of that spear. He easily cut through the soft tissue of the eye, and rapidly cut through the fleshly membrane and sinew, finally embedding himself to the hilt into the monster's brain. The force of the blow knocked the monster backward, killing it near instantly. As it fell to the floor with a loud thud, Seraph ran over to assist.

"Alexander, your ankles should be healed by now. You and Erin get over here!" Seraph yelled as he ran toward his father's unmoving form. His body was partially obscured and broken, embedded in the skull of the Gigas. "We need to get him out of there now! Alexander, give me a hand! Erin, try to brace his body when we pull!" Each man grabbed a leg and steadied the body with a hand underneath on the stomach as Erin, noticeably pale, waited to hold the body steady as it was pulled out.

Both men grunted as they dug their feet into the monster's back to pull Paul out, and with a sickening wet popping sound, they were able to pull him free. His chest rose shallowly; he was clearly severely injured. Likely from a punctured lung and broken ribs. He would likely live, though.

Seraph took it as a good sign to see that he was still breathing. Bit by bit they pulled more of Paul from the monster's skull. His torso had jagged bloody strips of flesh dangling and torn in thin pieces, ripped by the fragments of the monster's bone that had torn through his flesh. It was difficult to see, even for Seraph. Seeing the other two start to falter, Seraph spoke, "Keep moving.

We have to get him free. This is the dungeon; he's going to be OK. We just need to get him free so that he stops taking damage long enough to heal."

However, as they pulled his body out, it was hard to see how he was going to be okay. His dominant hand that had held the knife was now gone. Not cut off in that sense, but it had multiple breaks and was shredded as if all the force of the blow had been channeled through the arm. Upon hitting the back of the monster's skull, it had released into the arm and caused it to explode, unable to contain the kinetic energy. His face was bleeding badly, his forehead was cut, and bones showed through his face in multiple places from a whole host of deep lacerations and abrasions. Those kinds of injuries in the outside world would have likely already resulted in Paul's death.

"Keep his neck stable, Erin!" Seraph yelled as they finished getting him out of the Gigas' skull, laying him on the unbroken portions of the floor. Paul was unmoving and unresponsive. Seraph thought it was a small mercy that his dad was unconscious. He didn't need to be awake for this.

"Shouldn't we move on and try to find some medicine or something for him?" Erin asked. "I mean this is a school, or was, or is, I don't know, but maybe they have like a nurse's office?"

"Yeah, man," interjected Alexander. "He looks like he's in bad shape. We need to try to get him some help."

Seraph shook his head. "This is the dungeon. You need to throw away the idea of finding help here. As soon as we step through the doors, even if it's to look for help, it'll trigger whatever is next, or whatever monster is out there is going to start up or come our way. Are either of you prepared to help me fight another monster? Who's to say what we're going to find in those halls. It is best to wait and go as a complete and fully-healed team."

Erin looked at him in horror. "What do you mean wait. Paul is going to die. He looks like he's going to die. Isn't this your dad? How can you do that? How can you just let your dad die?"

Seraph looked down at his dad, worry evident on his face. "I don't want him to die, but if we step through that door unprepared, he will definitely die, and we won't be able to defend him if we get attacked. You're forgetting, and I keep telling you, this is the dungeon. So long as you're not dead, you will be OK. You will heal, so long as no monsters are around. It's why Alexander is able to walk right now."

"See, this is what I mean," Seraph said, pointing to his father.

Erin gasped, and Alexander called out "No way!" in shock at what they saw.

The bone and bloody pulp that Paul's arm had been reduced to began repairing itself, as blood and muscle tissue spawned within the arm, filling it out and restoring it, piece by piece. Gashes in his chest started to close up, and where there had been large wounds, they quickly became angry welts, and those welts eventually faded away to smooth skin. The flesh on his face repaired itself, and the bleeding soon stopped as his entire body rebuilt itself.

Within minutes, the damage to Paul's body was completely repaired, and with a gasp, he woke up. "Oh, wow, I'm still alive. That was the craziest thing I've ever done," he said, looking around at all of them. "Wow! I hurt all over. Why are you guys looking at me like you've seen a ghost? I couldn't have been that bad off, right?"

Seraph answered, "It's just amazing seeing how quickly the dungeon can heal wounds, that's all. We did it though, thanks to you. Our plan to cripple it beforehand ended up not working out so well."

Alexander cringed. "Yeah, sorry about that. I was hardly able to do anything."

Erin looked at him, her face still pale. "Are you guys sure he's OK? What if he's a zombie, or a ghost, or a monster? That's possible, right?"

Seraph frowned. He knew it was possible, but not in the sense that she implied. To become a zombie one had to be infected by a zombie, to become a ghost one needed to die while under a cursed effect, and to become a monster, one must renounce their humanity and be accepted by the dungeon. He answered simply, "He's not any of those things. He's alive, and this is a good reminder to all of you that so long as you don't die, you can survive pretty much anything the dungeon throws at you. We just watched his arm regrow in a matter of minutes. That's not an ability of his, that's the effect of the dungeon. It restores your health after each battle, so long as you're not around monsters or other enemies."

"That's interesting to hear," Paul said, "but do you guys mind helping me get my knife back? I'm kind of fond of it."

CHAPTER 11:
THE INFERNAL

The body of the Gigas started to smoke and bubble as soon as Paul mentioned looting the monster's corpse. Monstrous flesh rapidly rotted away as the nearby floor and bleachers quickly reassembled and rebuilt themselves from among the dust and rubble. The body rapidly decomposed until only an oversized grinning skull remained.

Everyone in the group looked on in awe as the dungeon rapidly repaired itself of the damage it had sustained until no hint of the recent carnage could be seen. To Seraph, for whom this sight had been far more common, it was not so amazing. It was just a fact of life within the dungeon. But for the rest of them, even after all they had seen already, it was still mesmerizing to behold.

With the corpse of the Gigas mostly

melted away, the only thing remaining was its skull. Leaving the group free to collect the drops. But as they combed the area, all they could find was Paul's knife—a knife that had been badly chipped and was bent in places with signs of catastrophic failure near the hilt of the blade. It was clear the weapon had suffered major damage and would no longer be useful. But as for the drops, they found nothing. For all the danger the group had put themselves in, and with the loss of a weapon, they had nothing to show for it. Each of them, even Seraph, had an expectation that the effort to kill the monster would be rewarded. Everyone looked at the handle of the broken knife and shot each other dirty and resentful looks.

The looks erased in mere seconds as the skull of the Gigas began to crumble into dust before their eyes once the broken knife had been removed from the eye socket of the skull, and in response, the entire group received a prompt.

Notification: Reward – To Kill A Gigas
Details: For defeating a monster beyond the average level of your party, each member is granted 2 stat points to use, and 3500 Sol to

purchase abilities directly from the shops in Hometown. This monster gives no experience.

Seraph mentally summoned his status screen to appear before him and instructed the other members of the group to also do so. He then went ahead and applied the two points he had just earned as a reward—one point to strength and one point toward endurance. He would have liked to put the points elsewhere, but the overall weakness of his body demanded that he devote the points toward strengthening core weaknesses. Seraph refused to fall behind.

Name: Luca Fernandez
Race: Fallen
Aliases: None
Passives Abilities
Body of Mana

Abilities
Thousand Handed 22-1000
Level: 4 of 999

Unassigned Stat Points: 0
Current Experience: 21-60

STR: 2 INT: 1 AGI: 3
WIS: 1 LCK: 1 PHY: 0*
END: 2 PER: 3
SOL: $03535*

The turn of events had a noted effect on the morale of the group, and though the over-all mood had soured before, the updated awards had blunted some of that. One thing that Seraph knew was that the current state of Paul's weapon would create issues. Logically, Paul was at best a liability. He was currently the second best fighter in their group, aside from Seraph, but without a weapon, this counted for nothing.

Everyone looked toward the open door and the darkness on the other side of it. No one moved to volunteer to be first to check it out, and no one should have to volunteer thought Seraph as he quickly assessed the group. The rest of them were all looking toward Paul to go in first, but not one of them moved to let him use their weapon.

If Seraph knew anything about people, it was that no group would accept as its leader someone who didn't lead from the front, and without a weapon, there was no way for Paul to do so. The group couldn't trust him to take point like he had before, even if he was still a top fighter. Now he was just an unarmed top fighter, and that mattered.

Seraph knew it was time for him to take the lead, and so he volunteered. "Don't worry about it, you guys," he said. "I've got this one. I'll go through first and then give the all-clear to follow. My eyes give me an advantage in the dark anyway. They're not just for show." The tension in the group eased a little—though only a little—after he volunteered.

Truthfully, neither did he, but some of his reservations were already fading as he started to feel the density of his muscles change as a result of his recent stat application. Even though increasing something by a single stat point seemed like nothing, it wasn't. It mattered, and he was already feeling stronger.

What many people didn't understand when they first entered the dungeon was that the initial starting value of 1 did not imply weakness, but rather their own subjective starting point. The base stat being modified by the additional stat points in an addictive fashion. For example, having a strength stat of 2 did not mean that a person's strength was suddenly doubled, it meant that their base strength would be increased by a small bonus—such as a person being able to lift 200 pounds with a base stat of 1, might be able to lift an additional 10 pounds per additional point of strength.

Supplemented by his body of mana passive ability, he had been able to overcome what would have been a crippling handicap to his stat advancement, but Seraph knew that when he had the chance, he would need to train his body to increase the value of his base. This was one way that true power within the dungeon was advanced.

Sometimes, as Seraph knew only too well, the only way out was through, so with all the confidence he could muster, Seraph pulled himself up, puffed out his chest, and took bold, confident steps toward the door. He didn't feel any fear. He knew he could take care of himself, but the people in his group needed to see some exaggerated confidence in hopes that some of it would rub off on them. He needed them to see him as somebody they wanted to follow.

Behind him, a loud ticking sound could be heard as the countdown clock within the gymnasium reset itself. Seraph wasn't worried about it; he knew the room was getting prepared for the next participants who would soon be coming through—though with the warped flow of time, he was unsure if that would be a matter of hours or days. What he did know was that they needed to leave before all the monsters they had already killed respawned within their midst. Seraph was unsure and could only guess whether the monsters respawned on a timer, or if they spawned upon entry into the gymnasium. It didn't really matter to him, as the ultimate consequence remained: if they lingered too long, the likelihood that they would be killed exponentially increased. The dungeon did not take kindly to those who did not progress, and something would force them to move or perish. It was a problem best left avoided and unexplored.

Notification: You are now entering "The Desolate High School". A safe zone has been designated ahead to be used as a rest area. Safe Zone "The Office".

He quickly dismissed the prompt. The first thing he noticed was the sudden change in the atmosphere. The surrounding air was noticeably colder and stagnant. For a brief moment, Seraph thought he could see his breath, but he realized he was mistaken upon discovery of a thick fog like gloom settling within the halls. The air was heavy with dust and cobwebs that made it difficult even with his eyes to see, but he saw no danger. He peered back and gave the signal to the group that he was OK—so far—and then he proceeded to walk up the stairs.

Being in the lead, he was able to use a technique as he walked up those stairs that he had not yet shared with them. A technique to supplement the senses. Seraph honed in on his eyesight, and as he focused, his vision became sharper and more defined. However, even with his dark vision, Seraph could not see well through the gloom. He shifted his attention and will away from his vision and toward his hearing, and as his vision dimmed back to normal, his hearing increased. In the distance, he thought he heard the scurrying of feet, but with the lack of light and low visibility, he couldn't see what he heard. From the sound of it, those scurrying feet were not too close, and they did not seem to be moving his way.

The only other sound he heard was the booming echo his own steps made as his boots left footprints in the thickly-layered dust, marking his passage on the stairs. The noise traveled far into the gloom—something he heard even as he released his hearing and returned it to normal. When he reached the top of the stairs, he stopped for a moment, just to make sure that it was safe before motioning to his skittish team members to follow him.

One by one, they entered the stairwell. Paul entered first, giving Seraph a thumbs-up from the bottom of the stairs, followed by Erin. As she began to ascend the stairs, she screamed in terror as cobwebs got into her hair, thinking a monster had grabbed her. Paul looked at her in irritation as he motioned with his hands that she needed to be quiet. Bashfully, she looked away in embarrassment. Alexander was the last to enter the stairwell, and as he did so, a door slammed shut behind him. A door that hadn't existed up until then. He turned to look through the window of the newly spawned doorway.

"It's dark!" Alexander called out in a hushed whisper, and then he tried the door. "It's locked too. We won't be able to turn back from here."

When all of them had finally reached the top of the stairs where Seraph had been waiting, a light turned on, automatically illuminating the area around them. They were at the end of a hall that led out in three different directions. A sign read "Office" above a door directly in front of them down the hall, while an old exit sign hung directly above them, pointing toward a locked double door. The hallway itself turned at the office and continued, though to where Seraph could not see.

The exit sign was no longer illuminated, and for Seraph that was a clue that the exit was not to be trusted. It was most likely just a trap to catch the unwary and unaware. A correct assumption it appeared, as Erin approached the locked exit and screamed "Monsters!" as she looked through the glass pane at the top of the door to what lay beyond.

Seraph rolled his eyes in annoyance. "Of course, there are monsters." He hissed. "This is all part of the dungeon experience. It is literally full of monsters, and every time you scream, fate rolls the dice and decides whether or not we get swarmed by them." She didn't respond as she continued to look through the window, her hands pressed against the door. As Alexander and Paul moved toward the door to also look, he felt obligated to follow, keeping his attention focused on the splitting hallway behind them.

Neither Paul nor Alexander screamed, but Seraph noticed fear etched on their faces. Not just on Alexander's, but on Paul's face too. That was something that had been lacking, even in the fight against the Gigas or when he faced the Kobolds. Seraph realized why when he looked through the windowpane and saw it. A vast Hellscape was visible among the ruins of what had once been a town. A green mist lingered. Everywhere he looked, all he could see were hulking monstrous abominations of ruined flesh roaming aimlessly past destroyed cars and rotting mutilated mounds of corpses. This was something that Seraph feared too. He knew what those things were, and while he had been able to kill them in the other timeline, he could do nothing to stop them now. The Infernals.

Seraph bent forward and whispered to them, "Slowly get away from the window, and stay away from those things out there from now on. Those things outside can kill any of us instantly. The Gigas was nothing compared to them." Paul noticed Seraph's fear and pointed to the door. It had been completely sealed, first by chain and then by what looked to be solder. For all purposes, at this point, it was a barrier—basically a wall, and a door no longer. Seraph breathed easier upon seeing that, but he still made the group move away as he saw one of the abominations drag a struggling body down the street by septic entrails. Even death was not an escape, Seraph noted.

As they moved away, Seraph was reminded of something. If this was the dungeon and not an actual place, then those monsters couldn't get inside, or at least they couldn't get inside easily. The dungeon wasn't immune to the incursions of the Infernals, but it did offer substantial protection from them. What Seraph didn't know though was if the Infernals outside were dungeon constructs. Were they still part of the tutorial, or were they the real deal? He had to assume the latter and hope for the former.

In a hushed whisper, Alexander asked Seraph the question that was on the mind of the rest of the group. "What are those things? Do you know? Are we safe?" They seemed to finally believe in him to an extent that he had some knowledge from the future, and in this case, he saw no reason to keep what he knew from them.

"Yes, I know of them. In my other life, we called them 'Infernals.' I am not sure what they are, or where they come from—much of their origins are unknown—but they are extremely dangerous. Warriors level 300 and above were killed by these things. When they first appeared, they spread across the entire surface of the Earth and killed every single person who was not inside the dungeon. The dungeon was the only place safe from them. There were very few things that could hurt me before I restarted. The Infernals comprised the majority of the things on that list," he explained.

"The answer of what to do is easy enough. We will just avoid them for now. It's good to know they exist, and we are safer in knowing that we need to avoid them at all costs," Paul added. "If this is part of the tutorial, they are out there either as a forewarning, or as a call in preparation to meet them one day."

As far as guesses go, it wasn't a bad one, mused Seraph in agreement. "I don't really know much about them. Even with foreknowledge, I've still got blind spots, and there are a lot of things I just don't know enough about."

Erin spoke up. "Maybe it's a clue. Things don't just get put out there in a setting like this without reason."

"What do you mean?" asked Alexander as Paul and Seraph looked at her, wondering the same.

Erin looked each of them in the eye and responded, "I know you don't like me. I'm not stupid, and because I'm not stupid, I do notice things. I do know things. If what you told us is true, then this whole thing is about preparing us for something that's to come. You told us those things out there eventually kill everyone. So, here's what I think. Either this is about providing clues on how to prevent that by showing us some way to fight those things, or it's about building up exposure to these Infernals so more people can be saved when the moment comes."

Seraph doubted it was about exposing people to the Infernals. Just simple exposure wouldn't save anyone. It was near impossible for regular people to plan ahead for something like that, and those things were simply beyond what regular people could manage.

"I think I've got it," mused Alexander. "This is part of some tutorial, right? So, if only people who enter the dungeon are shown those things out there, and only people still on Earth are killed by them, why would the dungeon show them to us? I think you're right Erin. It has to be the dungeon is trying to show us a way to fight those things. Somewhere in this building is the answer on how to defeat those things and save the Earth."

Seraph looked at him in shock as he spoke, and Alexander got a wide embarrassed smile, certain that he had messed up talking like he did out of turn. "You're absolutely right. Both of you," admitted Seraph. "There must be something here that we need to do before moving on —before using our tokens—and I'm willing to try and find it. Will you guys help me?"

They both nodded in agreement, and as Seraph turned to his father Paul for his opinion, he found the man was gone. A moment of panic set into his bones as he started to fear that something had taken his father. It was only for a second though as he saw Paul opening another door.

"What are you doing?" Seraph hissed.

Paul responded back with a pointed finger at the sign that said "Office."

Seraph nodded; it was as good as any place to start.

CHAPTER 12:
TRUE COLORS

Without a word between them, and creeping as quietly as they could, Paul, Seraph, Erin, and Alexander snuck into the office that had been designated as a safe place. Treading carefully so as to avoid attracting the attention of any monsters nearby, their bodies pressed against each other in a stack as they moved. Each of them was filled with trepidation, unsure about what they might find inside. Even Seraph felt the tension. The presence of the Infernals just outside the walls of the school was a danger none of them could handle. If one somehow managed to get into the building, he would be forced to abandon them, his father included.

Paul took the lead to open the door into the office, and on a whim, he checked to see if the light switch was working. To everyone's surprise, the office lit up, and when nothing moved, the remainder of the group followed Paul's footsteps, closing the door and securing the room behind them.

As they passed through the doorway, each of them had to resist the urge to gag as they were met with the hot and musty smell of stale air and old, rotted wood. It was clear that the people who had been here before had left in a hurry, as dust covered every surface, and then there was the moldy, spoiled remnants of food left out on the desks. Papers cracked and yellowed with age were sprawled everywhere, the counter space was cluttered with evidence of half-finished handyman tasks, and the receptionist's desk looked as if it had been roughly pushed away in haste. All evidence that an abrupt incident had likely come to this place.

Alexander went to open his mouth and say something but was stopped as Paul motioned to each of them to be quiet. He reached out and grabbed a claw hammer from within the handyman's belt that lay on the floor in front of the counter. Paul pointed to Alexander and motioned for the man to follow him. They would make sure the area was clear before everyone spread out to begin looking around. Seraph, having already led the way through the dark, was okay with the change in duties. He would stay behind and make sure nothing came through the office door behind them. His responsibility was to keep the space secure.

In just a few moments, Paul and Alexander came back from their security sweep.

"All clear. No signs of danger. Maybe this really is a safe area," Paul reported to the group as he allowed his posture to relax.

Alexander nodded his head in agreement. "I didn't hear or see anything either. This office is smaller than I thought though, it's just this space here, and then those two rooms over there. It looks like a nurse's station and then maybe the principal's office. I didn't see any other doors though."

"Good thinking, you guys," complimented Seraph. They were learning a bit. This wasn't the world that they were used to anymore. Adjusting to the new normal would be to their benefit, it would help with everyone's survival, and the more they looked out for themselves, the less Seraph would have to reveal himself.

"Alexander, give me a hand with this desk. We need to move it over there to barricade the door. It's the only way in or out of here, and I don't know about the rest of you, but I need to rest. I don't think I've ever been this tired, and I need to lie down before I completely crash," Paul said, his voice showing some of his weariness.

He did seem tired, noted Seraph as he looked at his father's face. He then turned to each of the others' faces. They all looked weary; fatigue was setting in already. Time worked differently in the dungeon, and it felt like days had passed—even though Seraph knew it had still only been a few hours since he had even talked Paul into entering the dungeon. But he also knew that if he was the last to have been transported into the gymnasium, the effect he currently felt was likely magnified for the others who had arrived earlier.

"I'll take first watch then," Seraph said as he volunteered, much to everyone's surprise. He noted the surprise in irritation and had to shove down his feelings of anger at their response. It made sense for him to be the first one to stand guard. He had been the last to arrive. *Did they not think somebody needed to keep watch?* he thought.

"I'll look around a bit and see if I can find anything we can use, or anything of importance. I'll make sure nothing bothers you guys while you're asleep," he explained. "This isn't your home, and this isn't a camping trip. You can't ignore the need for security."

They all looked embarrassed by what he said. Especially his father. *That answers it*, Seraph thought. *They didn't think anyone needed to keep watch over everyone else's sleep.* Seraph knew the look; it was the look of somebody who had known better. Paul had served in the military, where somebody was always on duty while everyone slept—especially when there was a threat of imminent danger. Here in the dungeon —with those things just outside, and who knew what inside—danger was close.

Paul started to protest, but he was interrupted by Seraph who replied, his tone heavy with irritation, "It's fine, Dad. It really is. I've been here the least amount of time. It's only fair that I can stay up a little longer so everyone can rest, even you. That healing you did earlier can take a lot out of you. I'm sure no one else has a problem with it. Try to rest, and I'll wake you if I need you."

Erin and Alexander both nodded their heads in agreement. Neither had a problem with Seraph taking the first shift so they could rest. Seraph could only smile inside as he knew how relieved both of them were to not have to stay awake and be the one on guard. People were so easy to manipulate sometimes.

Seraph listened carefully, drawing in on himself to expand the ability of his hearing as his vision and sense of smell decreased, but of the earlier scurrying sounds, he heard nothing. Waiting, he heard nothing shift in the dark. Whatever was out there wandering the halls wasn't currently moving. He released his hearing and took up a watchful posture, sliding dust off the chair of the receptionist's desk as the other members of the team slid down the wall, resting against it before nodding off to sleep.

Seraph didn't expect any of the members of his team to sleep deeply, so it came as a surprise that within seconds of them laying down, all of them were sleeping, even his father who had started to snore loudly. He had to remind himself not to judge too harshly. This was, by all means, a major life event. An event they were tolerating better than most.

For a moment, Seraph grew irritated in frustration that the noise they were making would draw other monsters to them, but he quickly dismissed it. He was confident that this area was under the jurisdiction of the dungeon, and as such, it had rules that had to be obeyed. One of those rules being that within the dungeon, it was impossible for adventurers to fall asleep, unless in a safe zone. This impossibility didn't extend to status effects, like passing out or being knocked unconscious. He didn't actually need to stand on guard, but it left him with time to search.

This fact meant they were safe, truly safe —at least, for a moment—and Seraph was free to look for whatever secrets this place had hidden from him. He would start with the contents of the receptionists' desks.

The center drawer was locked, so he moved on to the other drawers, finding in one a stack of paper reports showing current absences and class size. He put a few of the class reports in his pocket storage to show everyone else. As he rifled through the reports, he saw that there had been a drastic decrease in class size down to single digits by the year 2038. He looked, but he saw no further reports beyond that date. But then he hadn't expected any. 2038 was the year the green mist had spread over most of the world.

Taking a look at the reports, they were likely a clue, warning future adventurers of a coming calamity. *This is interesting*, thought Seraph as he considered the possibilities. Within the original timeline, he had never heard of any such warning, and he wondered if this was a change that had occurred because he had traveled back in time, or if it was a secret that had been waiting but had either never been discovered or disclosed in the original timeline. The latter he found problematic and would need to rule out that someone hadn't obscured the warning and kept it from him.

The picture of a woman and her daughter looked up at him from on the desk, and as he looked through the paperwork, he tried to ignore it. But something about the picture irritated him. He couldn't stand the way the family seemed to be looking at him. He reached out to turn the picture over, and on the other side, he found a key attached to the back of the photo— a key he guessed would likely fit into the center drawer that had been locked.

As he put the key in the lock, he knew he had been right in his guess as the lock turned. As he pulled out the drawer, he wondered what he would find. Fantasies about dungeon drops, rare loot, and stat boosts played out in his mind. Instead, all he found were paper clips, pens, a half-empty bag of hard candy, and a dated copy of Time magazine. *Actually,* he thought. *Maybe not useless after all.* He grabbed the bag of candy and the magazine and went to read.

As soon as he saw the cover he panicked.

His face, his actual face, was on the cover—not the childlike one he was currently wearing, but the face of his original body. The cover read in damning red ink. "Who's coming to save us? A look at the Crows and their enigmatic leader, Seraph, on page 11."

His heart pounded, and he looked at the others and saw they were still sleeping. He needed to do something about this. He couldn't just rip it out, though. The noise would definitely wake the others, and if the article contained even a fraction of his secrets, he would be forced to make sure the others never left here alive—even Paul. Some secrets needed to stay buried.

He quickly scanned the table of contents, seeing if there was something he might be able to use. *Ah, that will work*, he thought as he congratulated himself on his find. He moved the magazine, began to pull multiple pages out, and crumpled those remaining to throw back into the drawer.

The noise woke up Erin as the other two remained asleep.

"Hey, did you find something?" she asked in a groggy voice as she tried to rub the sleep from her eyes.

"Nothing spectacular so far," he lied. "Just

an article called 8 Ways to Best Delve. It'll be good to share with everyone as a reference and training manual when we finish this tutorial. I found that along with some other documents that kind of hint about what's going on here. I'm just not ready to divulge those quite yet though until I can figure out what it all means. Go back to sleep, though. I still have to look around some more. I'll wake you up when it's time for my shift to be over. I promise."

Erin nodded her head, her eyes already glossing over with drowsiness. Yawning, she said, "Alright, and thanks for doing this. I really appreciate it, and I bet your dad does too." Before she had even finished the last word of her sentence, she was curled up and resting against the wall, her eyes shut and sleeping soundly.

Without moving a muscle, Seraph waited to ensure that she remained asleep and that no one else had woken up in the meantime. He wasn't sure how long they would stay asleep, but he did not think it would be for long. They may not know it yet, but sleep during a delve in a designated safe area was always short.

Quickly, he searched the other desks but didn't find anything that looked or seemed important. Before leaving the room, he gave it one last look to see if he had missed anything, but nothing caught his eye before moving out.

There were two rooms he still needed to search. Both were at the back of the office, on opposite sides of each other, and down a short hallway. The first had a sign in a bronze plaque that read "Principal". He would visit that room last. The second door had a sign that read "Nurse's Office". Of the two, he had a suspicion that what he was looking for could be found in the principal's office, but a quick search of the nurse's office first would likely provide some loot.

As he flicked on the light, Seraph noted that it could hardly be called an office. More a small room with a clinical, industrial-looking bed. On the bed were two dusty boxes, and there was a small medical container on the wall that read "Emergency Kit."

"This will come in handy," he muttered as he grabbed the side of the container to take the emergency supplies. Inside the kit, he found a small bottle labeled "Pain Killers" and some gauze. Picking up both, he placed them in his spatial pocket.

Notification: You have acquired 2 pills. Each pill grants pain immunity for 5 minutes and restores health during combat to "Stable" status.

Notification: You have acquired "Set of Gauze".
Application of gauze cures "Bleed" status.

This was a good find. He would share one with Paul when he had the chance, but for now, he would keep both on him until a better time presented itself. The only thing left in the room was the two boxes on the medical bed, and the only thing left for him to do was open them.

Two identical boxes meant only one thing. One was real, and one was a fake, likely a mimic. The only way to know for sure was to either open the box and suffer massive damage or even loss of life, or to attack it up front and hope to kill the mimic first and not accidentally destroy the lot.

"Oh, well," he said with a sigh as he pulled his mace from the loop on his belt and swung down on the first box. The box screamed—a short sort of death knell—as his weapon struck, striking on soft flesh rather than cardboard. Black blood oozed from teeth where the lid of the box had been. Seraph felt instant relief that he had been correct in his guess, and from the lay-out of the teeth, he would have likely lost a hand if he had attempted to open the box.

Rapidly, the mimic began to shrivel up and decompose. In its place dropped a handful of the tokens to leave Phase II and begin Phase III. He quickly counted, and they almost had enough for everyone to pass on. He would divvy them out when everyone woke up. Carefully, just in case, he opened the second box and breathed in relief when this box didn't attack him. Within the box, he found a gold brooch that gave off a faint blue light. Seraph knew that the item was enchanted, but until he could get it identified, he would be unable to use it.

"Hey, what's that? We heard a noise and I volunteered to check it out so the others could go back to sleep. Something like a monster. Is everything OK?" came a voice from behind him. Seraph turned to see Alexander there. "I found a brooch and some tokens after killing a monster in a box," Seraph replied as he showed off the brooch, trying to pass off the item as something casual to minimize the extent of his find.

Alexander looked at the brooch with a disgusted expression. "Why are you carrying around a brooch? That's worthless. I'll make you a deal. I'll let you keep the brooch, and in return, you give me some of those tokens."

Seraph looked at him and saw that Alexander had maneuvered himself to block the doorway. He had no intention of letting Seraph get away without handing over the tokens. This was not how Seraph wanted to spend his limited time. "Sure, I was going to give them out anyway," he responded.

An idea came to him, and he counted out the full ten tokens and placed them in Alexander's hand, but rather than let go, he held on as Alexander looked at him with a brief expression of surprise and noticeable fear. "Activate," Seraph said to the tokens as he released Alexander's hand.

Instantly, Alexander disappeared. He would be a problem for later, but for now, Seraph had other matters to attend to.

CHAPTER 13:
LEFT BEHIND

Looking at the space where Alexander had been, Seraph internally reprimanded himself for being impulsive. This had been sloppier than he intended and would likely cause complications. Complications that he would need to deal with almost immediately, as well as complications in the far off future. He knew realistically that no explanation would fix this.

Even though Seraph had tried to remain quiet as he searched the safe area information and items, he had still been loud enough to wake up Alexander. He had made a mistake, and that mistake had likely been whatever noise had woken Alexander up, or that Seraph had been mistaken in his belief that Alexander had been peacefully sleeping when he went to search the back rooms.

Regardless, it was his mistake to own—and a reminder that his senses were not without flaws. He could be fooled; he could be caught unawares. It was an important reminder that he was not some primordial being, not some god incarnate, for now he was just a boy, or at least had the body and experience of one. With only a few things different, this would have been an exceptionally dangerous situation for him. He needed to get stronger much faster.

Thankfully, I was able to salvage the situation, he thought. *By sending Alexander onward, instead of being forced to try to kill him.*

The mechanic had not been difficult. All it had required was the active intent to use the tokens and the verbal command. A common technique he was familiar with from his other life. It was just a matter of will. Will and intent. Without a minor infusion of mana, the spoken command, and a will to activate the tokens, it would never work. This was a fail-safe to protect the new and uninitiated, but as Seraph had just done, there were still a few ways to abuse it.

Looking again at the empty spot, Seraph's thoughts turned back to Alexander. He knew little of the man. Their paths had not crossed in his first life. Seraph was sure Alexander had been an early casualty. The man's purpose was unclear, and though the man might not have been a genius or an expert fighter, he did show promise. Seraph preferred not having been forced to take the man's life. He was no necromancer; the dead didn't yet serve him.

That said, if Alexander had woken up or only pretended to be sleeping, it was possible that Erin or his father had heard the noise he made from slamming the boxes and would come to investigate or notice Alexander's absence. He was prepared. He had already thought of a story, ready and prepared if needed. Alexander was, after all, an oddity.

He moved silently to the doorway, careful to not make another sound, and he peered out. He couldn't see them sleeping from where he stood, but he could hear them. The sounds of soft sleep came from Erin, and from Paul, he heard loud snoring. They were asleep, though not where he remembered them falling asleep. They too must have woken and moved around. If that was the case, he still had time to keep searching before they woke.

Quickly—but not so quickly as to not be careful, or make more noise—he picked up the remaining tokens from inside the room. He had the ones still left in the box, and then the excess left behind from when Alexander's ten tokens were activated. Lastly, he reached for the brooch he had found and pinned it to his jumpsuit. As he was walking out he stopped himself as he realized he had missed something. He lowered himself to the floor and pulled a small metal washer from one of the corners of the medical bed. If one didn't look at it too closely, it resembled one of the phase advancement tokens. He quickly stashed it in his pocket, stood up, shook the dust off, grabbed the helmet, and left the room.

One never knew if some quick sleight of hand might be necessary. There were still no guarantees they would find enough tokens for those remaining to move on.

Looking around one last time to make sure he had grabbed everything, Seraph smiled to himself. This was his element, and while he wouldn't quite call it thriving, he was living, and soon he hoped he would find a way to unseal his power that lay in the Emblem of the Black Seraph.

They currently had enough tokens for two people to move on to the next stage at any time, and if he knew anything about his father, it was his father that would refuse to move on if anyone was left behind. But more so, he knew that if everyone could move on, most would choose to do so, and Seraph knew on an instinctive level that they needed to stay and explore further.

He thought of the small washer in his pocket that looked so much like a token. An insurance policy, if one was needed.

With only one more room to check—the Principal's Office—Seraph crept a few feet down the hall as quietly as he could. From Erin and Paul, he heard no sound or movement, and so he assumed they must still be sleeping. On some level, Seraph knew he was in conflict with his stated purpose of guarding them in their sleep, and he knew if they found out he wasn't doing that, it would not be well-received. But it couldn't be helped. He had no reservations about what he was doing. This was an opportunity to explore this place uninterrupted, without having to explain or think of more palatable explanations for why he knew things. He wanted to avoid questions he wasn't prepared to lie about or had no interest in answering.

Gently, he turned the bronzed doorknob and softly pushed the door forward, careful and slow to try to keep it from creaking and making too much noise, possibly waking one of them up.

What he saw stunned him. Unlike the general office space were Erin and Paul lay sleeping, the principal's office was meticulously clean and immaculate, as if someone, or something, had been here recently. There was no other explanation. It had the faint look, feel, and smell of having had recent exposure to the outside world. It was not stale and musty as the other rooms had been. But except for the footsteps of his group, there was no evidence that anyone else had even been here. The dust outside the office was further evidence that no one had been inside for years, if not decades.

Yeah, something isn't right here, Seraph thought as he gave the room a quick glance. The cleanliness was definite proof that this was the room he needed to dig through to find whatever secret this place was hiding. He pushed the papers on the desk aside and took off the brooch he was wearing and laid it on the desk. He wouldn't be able to benefit from it anyways until he got it identified, and for now, it was just getting in the way. But as he laid it down, he realized it was no longer giving off its previous blue hue of dim light, which meant it had been identified.

Seraph grabbed hold of the item and took a closer look at it.

Notification: Brooch of the Hometown Hero

– So long as you possess greater strength and agility than the other members of your party, you will be viewed as the leader of the group by non-members in the immediate vicinity.

He grimaced. It was a mostly useless bonus for him. It may have benefits, but he would likely trade it at the first opportunity rather than keep it. He had other ways to make people acknowledge him as a leader. He had hoped for buffs to his fighting ability, rather than charismatic bluffs. His had never been the way of the illusionist or the bard. What he did not gain through loyalty, he took through force. He would pawn it at first opportunity or toss it if it proved too inconvenient.

But this was not a revelation without merit. It was interesting that it had been identified, and the only way it could have been identified was if somebody on his team had done so, and he had already seen Paul's special ability, and he had seen Erin's ability, leaving the logical conclusion that Alexander had been the person to identify the item. If that was the case, Seraph found it interesting that Alexander had not tried to steal the item too.

At some point during their encounter, Alexander must have used an ability. An ability that he had previously refused to disclose. An ability that allowed him to identify items. Likely a non-combat ability, which was likely why he refused to disclose it before. The man was not just a fool, he was insecure too.

"Problematic," Seraph said to himself under his breath. "An insecure fool is a dangerous fool." There was little Alexander could have done to make himself less of a fool in Seraph's eyes. The man had attempted to coerce him, and ultimately, Seraph would ensure he paid a high price for that. Within the dungeon, the only thing that mattered was strength and the application of power. The dangerous nature of the dungeon cared little for anything else, but the people who lived in it cared about the actions of others and how those actions affected them. To Seraph, Alexander was as dangerous as a sword in the hands of an amateur.

Seraph dismissed the thoughts from his head because he needed to focus on the task at hand and finish looking through the office. He grabbed the stack of papers he had pushed aside when he laid the brooch down, careful to avoid knocking over the computer, and he quickly riffled through the paper, catching bits and pieces of what was written on them as he rapidly scanned them. In the piles of paperwork, he found nothing of importance—janitorial needs,

maintenance reports, aging equipment, old service authorizations, class progress reports, and
budget line items.

An old photograph on the corner of the
desk caught his eye, and he picked up the frame
to look at it. It showed a man in a crisp suit holding a woman in his arms. From the warm way
the man held her, Seraph mused it was likely his
wife, but both his face and hers had been torn
out. However, like everything else in the room,
the frame was not marred by fingers, grime, age,
or dust.

A chill ran down Seraph's spine. This was
proof that they were not alone in here, and from
the photograph, he had to assume that whatever or whoever else was here, they could freely
move about without leaving signs of their passing. Seraph was unsure how such a thing could
happen if they were in a safe area. The whole
chain of thought made him nervous, and the hair
on the back of his neck stood up.

He ran quickly to the office door and
looked out, his heart pounding. He was able to
get himself settled once he saw that the door to
the general area was still barricaded. Paul was
still sleeping, as was Erin. He promised at the
least he would pay more attention to their safety
and not completely ignore their situation, so

long as it did not interfere with his own mission.

Still, something was missing

He gave the room another look. The poster of Einstein on the wall didn't seem that relevant, and neither did the complete collection of Encyclopedia Britannica. He moved around to the other side of the desk, looking for drawers that he could open and check, and he was disappointed when he saw that there was only an empty steel shelf built into the interior of the desk, save for a short stack of post it notes that was almost depleted—an obvious sign of extensive use. Behind the shelf, he saw a long cord trailing down.

The computer, of course, Seraph thought. *The thing I'm missing.*

Seraph had forgotten the importance of computers; it had been a long time since he had needed one. He sat down in the chair, and after looking for a second to find the power button, he turned it on.

Notification: You lack the requisite intelligence to use this terminal. Requires 8 INT.

Notification: The skill "Tech Savvy" or "Computer Literate" is required to use this computer.

Irritated, he dismissed the prompts and turned the computer off. There would be other ways to solve this. He needed to find something out of place, something that didn't belong. Something in this room was the answer. He looked at the bookshelf again, going shelf by shelf, and just when he was ready to give up, he finally noticed something on the top of the bookshelf. A place he had not looked before, there was a white 3-ring binder with post it notes sticking out of the sides. He reached up and grabbed it, pulling it down and laying it out on the desk.

The cover was beat up, partially torn, and covered in greasy hand prints. The opposite of the room, it read across the top "Findings from the Mist's Edge - A Case Study by Reverend" and the top corner bore a mark that was secret to many but well known to Seraph. Three slash marks in each direction, the mark of Carrion Crow. It was the guild he had founded, the guild he had led into the abyss of the final floor, the Locum Malificar.

CHAPTER 14: THE WORMWOOD REPORT

Seraph gently opened up the binder, afraid to damage what he himself viewed as a precious artifact. The report was something from another timeline that had somehow managed to make it back into the past, just like he had. It was something that would tell him of the fate of Reverend, and ultimately there might be some clue or hidden knowledge that would help him in his mission to strengthen both humanity and himself.

The binder cracked as dust fell off in heavy clouds, the binding stiff with age as he turned to the first page, and then the second, and then the third. Every page was the same; every page was empty. But rather than being angered, he smiled, a sense of relief flooding him.

Reverend did his work well and had set upon the report the mandated guild measures for secrecy. Few in the other timeline could have ever read the report, and none but Seraph could read it now.

Seraph closed the binder, grimacing as it cracked as he closed it, and then he put his thumb on the guild mark hidden discreetly on the corner of the binder. The mark responded to him and the blood in his veins—a blood he had once shared with every elite member of his guild.

His thumb pressed harder against the binder; the guild mark warmed beneath his finger, and he repeated the words he had himself dedicated to the task of secrecy. Words he had demanded that others must always use and always keep secret.

Seraph spoke low in hushed tones, his words laced with mana and tinged dark with hints of his power, and his voice directed at the guild mark.

He spoke the keywords that he had long ago chosen for his guild and its members to use.

"It is written. Be loyal to the nightmare of your choices."

The guild mark glowed a crimson red and disappeared, fading out of existence. Nothing more than a tool of the guild to pass information in a coded fashion.

The binder quickly transformed into a small book with a leather binding. Eagerly, he opened it. This time the pages moved easily without tarnish or age, smelling heavy of fresh ink and newly cut leather. He quickly flipped to the first page and began reading the familiar handwriting that he recognized as belonging to Reverend.

"February 18th, 2048

This Tuesday marks the passage of six months since I first began my mission to further investigate the miasma that is spreading rapidly across the Earth.

Though they call it miasma, I do not. It is closer to a poison, a curse. It is a blight on the land and all it touches. With careful diligence and preparation, I have explored the border and been troubled by what I have found.

Of the monsters within I have seen little

directly, though I have seen evidence of incursions —tracks in the ground and dragging indentations leading from within the miasma to scattered homes near the border and back again into the miasma.

The monsters within seem to congregate closer to population centers. I have used this fact to conduct various research.

I used many different instruments to try to collect soil samples, but all except the iron collection tool rapidly corroded before my eyes. The single soil sample I took was fallow and hostile to life. Everything save the iron I used to collect it with corroded and turned necrotic.

Against my better angels, I reached into the miasma covered in iron and found the protection insufficient. The exposed flesh of my left hand became alien to me, becoming necrotic and necromorphic as my hand rotted. I quickly withdrew and severed the limb, which in turn I saw spawn additional limbs and scurry away.

I did not attempt further information collection. I have since replaced the limb with animated necromantic tissue, dead man's bone, and a minor illusionary spell. I have found much to my misery that this hand I have created for myself has a persistent effect of death touch. I must be careful.

Though my guild has ample resources that

could have benefited the mission, I made the decision to self-refer to this forward deployment to the contested outer regions without permission or further authorization. If successful, I know my master will forgive the liberty I have taken to further explore what we call the miasma, and what I call wormwood, for it is blight and the enemy of all life.

The infrastructure in the nearby towns has fallen into disrepair, and the roads are filled by both highwayman and refugees. Long throngs of hopeless people are traveling to wherever they believe they may find safety. The strongest among them hold their heads a bit higher. They all know the dungeon to be safe, and they know they may be allowed where only the strong are allowed to enter. It is not my place or duty to judge them and send them forward or dispatch them and end their journey. I have other purposes.

The dead are numerous, though most of the dead I have come across have fallen by the blade of the desperate hand and not by illness or monsters from the dungeon. Though I imagine for the dead it matters very little how or who killed them. Of those dragged into the miasma, I can make no assumptions if they are alive or dead.

I have so far been unsuccessful during my tenure here in finding a more appropriate cover for my actions and purpose within the area. Of work there has been very little. I have been forced to assume the mantle of interim principal of this high school.

It has not been terrible. Many of the conditions I had feared might cause others to be suspicious of my purpose have been mitigated by the extraordinary circumstances of the immediacy of the nearby miasma border. Many of the locals and elders within the community have long since fled, taking with them their families. Those who have remained are too poor, too sick, or too infirm to travel. As I shift through reports, I can see how every day fewer and fewer students remain.

Of the students who are left at the school under my care, I must say they have remained resilient and hopeful. A force I can barely register seems to be driving them with a will to survive. Though they have been left behind, I cannot act in accordance with guild tenets. Even in the coldest region of my own heart, I cannot do what duty demands of me. Even more so when the truth is evidence; I am all these children have. I have been unwilling even in the coldest region of my heart to find the strength to look at these children, look them straight in the eye, and tell them plainly that no one is coming to save them, and their loved ones have abandoned them.

I will not be that monster. Though I know on many levels, these children know and understand they have been abandoned. I believe there is no further purpose in chasing greater heartache. It is a small mercy I can give them to not mention this. These students who are left in my care, I cannot leave them. They are the left behind, those whose families could not afford to move them and absconded without them.

I have set up a shelter for these children in the main break area, and at night I tell them stories about happier times before the miasma and before the crows came. Most sleep peacefully with the lies I weave for their comfort. It is likely we will all be dead soon; I will not add to their misery or sorrows. Though the numbers of students in the school has dwindled over time, it has still been a heavy burden to bear. Soon I will bear it alone. I have seen the aids and the teachers, their eyes heavy and alight with fear, twitching and ready to depart at a moment's notice. Their gaze heavy with guilt, they cannot look at me, and they cannot look at the children. I fully expect to wake up soon and find the lot of them to be gone having fled. By nature there are few options available to them; I cannot find fault in it. I will not condone another's decision to live, just because I have made a decision that prepares me for death.

I have sinned against my master. That I care for these children, that I am their caretaker and by rights have sapped my own strength to care for them, is considered a grand heresy by the Guild of Crows, and only equally grand results would result in forgiveness and a pardon of weakness for these children. By all rights I should abandon them and report only on what I have found, but I cannot. I cannot leave them. I have grown close to them. As the miasma approaches, coughing can be heard down the hall, a sign that the air inside the school has already begun to foul. I will not leave these kids behind and that means there's only one hope for their salvation.

I have planted a single dungeon seed I found early on within my time in the dungeon. I have planted the seed into the very foundation of the school, and while I have felt the stirrings of influence of the dungeon below me, it has not yet sprouted. It is my hope that it shall grow and eventually envelope this school that I love, extending its protection to these children whom I cannot and will not leave behind. I know first-hand the strength that the dungeon can grant to those within it.

Whatever infirmities and weaknesses these children may have, I know they will be rectified once inside the dungeon. I cannot lead them through the known dungeon entrance. I will not lead them to be slaughtered mere meters away from salvation for things outside of their control, for faults not their own, just due to the capricious and malevolent nature of the Crows.

I hear screaming outside and faint sobbing. It appears I am out of time. A teacher knocks on my door asking for guidance on what to do, but I have none. The miasma has never moved this fast before, and from my window I can see it encroaching —not in mere centimeters and inches, but in miles. It is evident it will soon be here. I tell the teacher to gather the staff and the children and take them to the break area. Be kind, tell jokes, and be easy on them.

The teacher paused for a second, asking if I'm coming too, but I am busy. One by one, I unbutton my polished suit that has marked my authority within the school, a suit of heavy polished obsidian armor beneath it. I will soon grab my gauntlets and war hammer. I do not know how much my life will be worth, but I will spend it gladly for a few more minutes of life for these children.

I shall leave behind these findings in the hope that one day my master will find and benefit from them—and through him all of humanity—in fighting off this miasma I suspect to be wormwood.

Signed, Timothy Reverend

7th Seat of the Order of Crows

Guild officer of Carrion Crow

"The Earth Shaker"

Seraph looked down at the binder, his eyes heavy in an unfamiliar way as tears dropped on the white paper below. He was proud of the man who had been his friend, and remorseful of how his own actions and policy had likely caused his death. He wiped the tears from his eyes and compartmentalized the information. Information heavy with implication that he would need to save and bring up with the guild once they were established. In this information was a chance that Reverend had saved the human race with his research.

Notification: Discovery of "Wormwood"
Details: You have obtained information on the miasma in the report by Timothy Reverend.
He suspects it is something called wormwood.

Find a way to fight or ward off this wormwood by February 18th, 2048, or lose control of the surface area of the Earth and all who live upon it.

He closed the leather book, not bothering to reactivate the seal, and stashed it on his person, leaving the office much the same way that he had found it. He closed the door behind him in reverence to the man who had worked in it. Only a few minutes had passed since he had gone in, but he felt he needed a minute to think. He slumped down near the sleeping forms of his still-snoring father and the light snores of Erin.

As he looked at the wall, thoughts heavy on his mind, he wondered who he was. He called himself Seraph, but was he really? Could he really be? The thoughts of his old friend and subordinate lay heavy on his mind. If he was still Seraph, would he have this feeling of guilt and sorrow? He didn't know. He propped himself against the wall and waited for the others to wake up, watching as the hours passed and the thoughts in his mind remained troubled and chaotic.

CHAPTER 15: THE TIES THAT BIND

His wings flexed instinctively—a telltale sign of inner turmoil and anxiety that only those closest to him had ever managed to figure out. It was not a trait he readily revealed, standing in stark contrast to his well-groomed image of cold and harsh stoicism. He was anxiously waiting for news from the forward team, but he was more anxious to hear from Elle.

Rubbing his temples to relieve some of the tension he felt, he then clenched his fist in rapid succession as he worked the stress out of his body. Leadership was a trial all of its own. He looked at the rapidly updating map in the command center, feeling overwhelmed in a way he never had done before. That map marked the remnants of humanity on Earth. A sense of longing and bitterness fueled his thoughts as he wished for the simpler days when

Carrion Crow was just a killers' guild, not beholden to the responsibility of ruling the survivors.

"Heavy is the head that wears the crown," he muttered to himself as a voice from across the room tore him from his thoughts.

"Seraph, you need to see this!" shouted Zoldos, his voice tinged in regret as his arms moved faster than the human eye could see. His movement was a blurry whirl, giving him the illusion of at least partial invisibility. A trail of green in the air as he worked to update the map with his empowered stylus was all that was visible.

Seraph moved away from his command station and over toward the command node Zoldos was assigned to. He watched Zoldos' arms move faster and faster as more and more of the over-head map was updated, filled with green to match the miasma on the surface as it spread and consumed. It was a regret Seraph had in putting Zoldos to work in this place. Seraph had always enjoyed watching the man's knife work, and unfortunately for him, the quickness of his hands extended to his work in command node, which was exactly what Seraph needed.

By the way Zoldos held himself, the tone of his voice, and how he phrased those words, Seraph knew he needed to brace himself for bad news. He had a self-enforced policy that his subordinates could never see him react poorly or complain about *bad news. But today might be different. There was news he had been fearing all day, and even something as strong as him had things he feared.*

"It's the team, Seraph," said Zoldos, his head unmoving, centered and focused on his tasks of keeping the command center updated on all the incoming information, the blur of his arms in motion never stopping.

Seraph's heart stopped. He knew what that meant. No one ever stopped him during a crisis to give him good news, only ever poor outcomes and bad news.

"What about the team, Zoldos?" Seraph asked, his tone icy and yet devoid of any of the emotions currently raging inside him.

"They're gone," came the reply as Zoldos pointed to the guild roster on his command node. Seraph's eyes scanned the screen, and highlighted in gray, marking the deceased, were three new ones to join hundreds of others. New names: Elle, John, and Ken. Their time of death stamped next to their names, mere seconds between each.

"They're gone." Simple words, but he knew everything that it entailed. The team he had sent to scout the final floor of the dungeon had been com-

pletely wiped out. Whatever killed them had been monstrous enough to overwhelm three of his elites with enough speed and violence of action to prevent even one of them from escaping. He looked at the list again. Elle had died last. Maybe she had at least tried to escape the monster that came for them.

He clenched his jaw in anger. More friends lost, more comrades lost, and all for nothing. They knew nothing more about the final floor. Nothing except death waited for them there. Death waited just through the doorway marked Locum Malificar.

"They will be remembered," was all Seraph said as he turned away and headed back to his command desk. There was disappointment evident on the faces of the few subordinates that had overheard the exchange and his underwhelming response, wondering between themselves how he could care so little. Never knowing, and never guessing that Seraph's instinct and response was the urge to kill and massacre until his anger faded. To fill the empty space with tides of blood. Underwhelming kept his people safe from him.

"Wait, Seraph, it wasn't just the team," started Zoldos. "We've lost contact with most of the forward elements on the surface. The teams on the outskirts are reporting the miasma is moving again,

faster than they've ever seen it. The government is pulling out of D.C. They're all heading here, Seraph. They mean to take the dungeon from us. This is it. It's over."

That the government was pulling out of D.C. and thought they could actually take control of the dungeon was laughable. That was a confrontation Seraph was looking forward to. He alone could kill the entire lot of them. It didn't matter if they numbered in the thousands or tens of thousands, Seraph was on a level they would never reach. Communication was heavily restricted with the surface, and few knew what he was truly capable of. No one outside of his guild had lived to see what he could accomplish.

As for the rest of the world, Seraph mentally dismissed the news. He had largely given up on them; the green mist would soon come for them all, and only those strong enough to resist would remain.

"Seraph, there's more. I think you're going to want to suit up and head out after this," continued Zoldos as he turned around and looked Seraph in the eye.

"Alright, man. Hit me with the bad news," Seraph said as his wings bowed, bracing himself as he slumped against his chair.

Hazy green light filtered into the office, shining through the glass, and through the miasma that hung heavy just past the front doors. Though the change in light may have marked the passage of time, no one knew for certain, as the sun could not be seen. Inside of the school remained mostly dark, save the main office.

Curled up against the wall, the marks of dried tears marking his face through dust and grime, Seraph slept. And not the easy sleep of exhaustion, but the troubled sleep of the damned.

The filtered green light didn't wake him, and neither did the movement of bodies around him as his companions each woke up and moved about. Nor did the first kick wake him as it barely registered in his foggy mind, while the second kick jolted his senses into groggy awareness.

By the time the third kick came around he was fully awake, catching the kick and trapping the leg with a hold as he prepared to break the limb. He glared in furious anger over being disturbed, and he was more furious at whoever dared to attack him. Seraph's body becoming filled with power as wrath fueled his heart of darkness ability boosting his strength far beyond that of a man.

"Good. You're awake," Paul said, looking

down at him, his eyes heavy with judgment and posture equally telling, and his face uncomfortable with strain as he tried to pull his leg loose, pretending to not feel any pain as his leg began to fracture.

Seraph relaxed a bit upon seeing it was his father, his adrenalin subsiding and with it the majority of his anger. Though still noticeably angry, as his wrath abated so too did his strength. He relaxed his hold on the limb before freeing it all together, but the glaring continued as he looked away to wipe the dust from his face and erase the evidence that he had been crying.

If Paul noticed the tears he didn't say anything; instead, he was focusing on the hard look Seraph seemed intent on giving him. Paul spoke, his voice sharp and accusing, "I don't know why you've got that look on your face, kiddo. If anyone should be upset it's me and Erin. You were on guard, and you went to sleep without waking your relief. If you were that tired, you could have woken me up. I would have taken over—it wasn't a big deal—but falling asleep on guard *is* a big deal. I know you never served, but I can tell you, that's a hard no. You can't do that; lives depend on it. Literal lives."

Seraph looked away from Paul. The edge in his father's eyes was uncomfortable for him, grating on his nerves, and the logic behind it was not something he could easily argue away because it was true. He had fallen asleep. But he had fallen asleep in a designated safe zone. Whatever the danger outside, it didn't matter as the dungeon had always honored safe zones.

No, forget it. He looked back at Paul and matched the look. Whatever his father might think, there was far more at stake than his pride and sense of duty as a father—or whatever this was—and though Seraph kept reminding him, Paul kept forgetting that Seraph had lived decades longer than him already. Even if his body was still that of a teen.

As Seraph looked into Paul's eyes, he knew the truth of things. The truth he had been ignoring. A truth he could feel deep in his bones. Whatever bond of teamwork and companionship between them had once existed, it was now severed—if it had ever even truly existed.

He knew the half-truth of the lie of his resurrection was already unraveling. Not because of its lack of believability, but because of the over familiarity the others had toward him. He was young in body only, having already outlived both of them in the other timeline, and though his current hands and body were unscathed and unbloodied, his past self had waded through rivers of blood and survived not just one battle, but an innumerable number of battles over the decades.

As Paul's glare bore into him, his face contorted in anger as he impatiently waited for a response from Seraph.

Pathetic, he thought as he decided to say nothing, shifting his eyes to the remaining member of their party, Erin, and in her gaze, she held the same edge as his father. Her eyes were darting back and forth between him and Paul, searching for his father's approval. Within those eyes was a familiarity that hinted of more between them than just the shared trauma of their current experience.

"When did they have time for that?" mused Seraph.

Seraph shook his head in disgust, his face heavy with judgment of the two as they barely concealed their recent pairing.

"Hey!" interrupted Paul. "Look at me. Don't look at her for an out! Look at me. I'm the one that's your dad." It was clear to Paul that Seraph knew his secret, that something had happened between him and Erin, and the look of judgment on the boy's face infuriated him.

Erin reached out a calming hand toward Paul and finished the thought. "It's because one of us is missing, Luca. We can't find Alexander, and you were the last one awake. The last one to see him. We're just worried from when we woke up and went to find him."

Ah! thought Seraph, his face without emotion and showing no response to what they were saying. *That explains it. That explains all of it. They're suspicious of me. They must think I've done something to him or let something happen to him.* Not completely a huge leap to make certainly, and it was true. He had in a sense disposed of Alexander by sending him to the next phase of the tutorial, but they didn't need to know all of that.

"Yeah, he left on his own," explained Seraph. "I was the last one to see him. He waited until you were all asleep and all but jumped me as I was searching through the nurses' room back there for anything we might use. I was able to keep the medicine and the helmet I found, but he took the tokens from the room and left us behind."

Paul and Erin looked at each other for a

moment. The story sounded plausible enough to not question it too heavily. It was enough for Paul, and Seraph noted his father didn't look like he had anything further he wanted to say.

It was Erin who first broke the awkward silence that had fallen between them all. "So, he just what? Grabbed them and took off?" she asked.

"Well, no, not really," replied Seraph. "First, he checked to see if I had found anything he wished to steal and take with him, and then he took the tokens I'd found and moved on. Important distinction. He tried to rob me first."

Her gaze grew more suspicious, and Seraph decided not to press further with his story. Meanwhile, Paul went to the nurses' room to see if the story checked out as Seraph had described it.

"Maybe you're right. I see his footprints going into that room alongside yours. There are two boxes on the bed. I'm guessing that's where you found the tokens and the helmet you were talking about. Did you find anything else?" he asked.

"I did. When I was in the principal's office, I came across this report." Seraph said as he quickly stood up, and Erin recoiled from him as he reached into the interior of his overcoat, touching the guild mark as he did to reactivate the glamour placed upon the report. Instead of pulling out the leather book, he pulled out the far bulkier grime-covered binder and placed it on the counter for them to view.

Erin reached out to grab it, as Paul stood behind her and peered over her shoulder to read it. "This is just blank papers," they both said in unison, clearly annoyed by what they thought was Seraph playing games with them. It was not lost on Seraph that suddenly Erin and his father were a team working together, nor was the way they seemed to be gravitating toward each other. He would need to do something about that. Women could be a distraction, and Seraph did not need his father distracted.

"It didn't use to be" Seraph said as another lie easily flowed from his lips. "When I came across the report, I promise you that it wasn't blank paper. It was written by somebody named Timothy Reverend, in a version of the future that has yet to come to pass. He was the principal of this school, and his job was to study the green haze outside. He referred to it as a miasma, but also as 'Wormwood'. When I was done reading it, the words on the pages disappeared."

Erin looked at him suspiciously, but Paul

just nodded his head, questions prepared. "Why did he need to study that? When we first got here, you called those things out in the green mist Infernals right? Wouldn't that be dangerous for him?"

Seraph nodded. "It would absolutely be dangerous. His report read that he actually lost his hand when he reached into the miasma. He said he was forced to sever his arm, and when it fell to the ground it actually sprouted legs and walked away on its own."

The two adults both shuddered at the thought, likely thinking of vivid images in their head of spider-like appendages on a walking, severed limb. It was not the most pleasant of thoughts.

"Well, that horrifying disclosure aside, did you learn anything else?" asked Erin.

Seraph nodded. "I did. This Reverend wrote that he had planted something called a dungeon seed within this school, in hopes, I'm guessing, to get the school under the influence of the dungeon and maybe try to connect this place to the main dungeon hub to evacuate the students."

"Was he successful?" asked Paul. "Did it work?"

Seraph could only shake his head for now before answering. "I don't think so. I have no memory of his success, and this is the first I've heard of planting a dungeon seed. I've my guesses about what that means, but I'm pretty sure we need to find it. What's more, I don't think we're alone here.

"What do you mean, alone here?" Paul questioned. "Do you mean we're not alone here, as in there are more monsters like those we saw back in the gymnasium?"

"I wouldn't rule out more monsters, not even for a second, but that's not what I meant," replied Seraph. "What I mean is the people who were left behind, I think are still here. What I read heavily implied that when the green miasma spread this far, the kids who were still going to the school sheltered here. The principal was their caretaker, and their families abandoned them."

"What? That doesn't make any sense, Luca," interjected Erin. "Why would their parents just abandon them? Did things really get that bad?"

Seraph shook his head and ignored the

continual, casual use of his real name. Instead, he looked at Paul. "What I read said the kids weren't abandoned by their parents for safety reasons. What I read said the kids were abandoned by their parents because they were handicapped or their parents just didn't have enough resources to keep them alive. The principal—this Reverend—had been their caretaker."

Paul clenched his jaw and ground his teeth at this revelation, his fists clenched in anger, and his body showing signs of irritation. As a parent of a handicapped child who until very recently hadn't been able to walk, he had zero sympathy toward those who would abandon their children. But whatever angry thoughts he had he kept to himself, his body language said more than enough. In that contradiction of behaviors, Seraph found confusion.

"Alright. So, what are we supposed to do about it? Shouldn't we just try to find more of those tokens and move on?" asked Erin.

"We look for them," Seraph replied with cool indifference. "If they were left behind, they might still be here, and if we can, we save them."

Seraph didn't truly think that the students who had been left behind were still alive, but he did expect to likely find their bodies. It would take nothing effort-wise to take care of the bodies and put them to rest—a venture that he was positive his father and Erin would support. A venture that would let him further explore without the hindrance of his companions second guessing his motives, while also allowing him the presence of allies to minimize his personal risk. What he needed to do was find the dungeon seed.

"If you're so interested in risking your life, you can go first," said Erin mockingly as she motioned toward the door.

"I agree with Erin," Paul added quickly. "We should just look for these tokens and be gone. I don't think it's safe here anymore, in this graveyard—or whatever it is."

Seraph looked at one and then the other, a brief look of surprise on both of their faces as he pushed past them. He didn't have time for this, and whatever internal debate Seraph may have been having about whom to kill and not kill, this woman had condemned herself. She wasn't going to be leaving this place; she had become a liability.

As he opened the door to step out into the hall, hands shot out and pinned him to the wall. His father's hands. Seraph, with a cool look of indifference in his eyes, looked into his father's face, contorted, red, and ugly with anger yelling,

"What the hell is wrong with you?"

Seraph didn't respond. Scum like this didn't deserve an answer. As he jerked his body to get free, his father applied even more pressure to keep him in place, the veins in his arms starting to bulge as he strained his muscles. "I'm still your dad. You can't just do whatever it is you want to do. I won't allow it. No son of mine is going to act this way."

Rage flooded through Seraph's veins as once again his physical prowess was multiplied by the power of his dark heart ability. As the power flooded his body, so too did his awareness. He grew in stature and in build. Seeing the changes, Paul recoiled in fear and withdrew his hands from his son's body as elsewhere a glow of white light began to build up as Erin tried to back Paul up.

Thinking the matter settled, Seraph turned to leave, only to see his father spring forward in an attempt to tackle him to the floor. For Seraph it was a confirmation of how little they valued his opinion. His father may have served in the military, but what was a few years in the Army versus a lifetime of combat in the dungeon. Seraph's hand coiled into a fist, and he threw a vicious hook that connected with his father's jaw, sending the man sprawling unconscious to the floor of the office. If Paul had still been a regular human, the punch would have killed him instantly, severing his brain from his spinal cord and rupturing all of his internal organs from the impact as the kinetic energy dispersed throughout his body. Instead, the man would sleep it off, and in a few short hours, his body would finish repairing the damage, and he would wake up.

Seraph pulled out ten tokens for Paul to use once he woke, for, whatever came next, they would be going their separate ways. In spite of everything, Seraph did not want his father to die.

As he finished placing the tokens down, the white light that had been building up finally exploded. It was a light that blinded all of those who saw it, except the caster—in this case, Erin. As she approached Seraph, her body trembled in fear, but armed with her Cat's Claw, she was ready to strike him down. When her attack swiped at air where previously he had been, she could only gasp as ghostly arms reached out and grabbed her, arms of ethereal mana energy that didn't just grab at her body, but at her soul.

"What's going on? Let me go! Let me go! I don't want to die! I don't want to die!" she screamed.

"You just tried to kill me. Why would I let

you go?" answered Seraph. "You didn't listen to me when I told you I'd been here before. I've seen tricks like yours before. All I did was look away —not that it mattered. With how loud you're breathing, and how heavy your fear is, I could hear and smell you regardless."

"You're a monster. You may think you've got everyone else fooled, but I saw right through you. You're a monster; you're a stone-cold killer. I've known men like you. I know what you are." But seeing his hardened face, Erin changed her approach crying "Just please, let me go. I won't say anything,".

"No, that won't do," he replied. "You see, I am a monster, and I am a killer—something I'm reminded of right now as my thousand arm ability keeps you immobile. What you don't seem to understand is that I value a little discretion— discretion you haven't shown. I have a mission I won't let anyone interfere with—something that you've just tried to do. So, if nothing else, thank you."

"Thank me? For what?" she asked, fear evident on her face."

"For this," Seraph responded as he tore her soul from her body and consumed it, gaining her ability. "And for this," he told her lifeless body as he equipped the Cat's Claw.

CHAPTER 16:
LOOSE ENDS

Notification: You are "Fatigued." For the next 5 minutes you will be unable to move while your stamina recovers.

Heavy breathing echoed down the hall from the interior of the office as Seraph collapsed onto a knee in complete exhaustion from the fight with the two adults. His stamina and his mana were completely depleted, leaving him in near paralysis from fatigue. He was unable to move or defend himself.

He let out a short, manic laugh, amused that he had been brought so low by something so simple. Even his body of mana passive ability had been disabled. There was a time in that other life when he would have simply killed someone for showing the same sort of weakness he was showing now. A silent thanks went out that the only danger to him currently was likely far down the hall, and his stamina would probably recover before any monsters could reach him.

Though Seraph was fairly positive nothing moved in the dark toward him in response to his labored breathing. He couldn't be sure, and in his current state he lacked the ability to focus any of his senses to determine if something was after him.

The rapid use of his abilities had left him drained. His low stats were a liability, as shown by his exhaustion from the brief confrontation with his father. Though he no longer possessed the body or abilities of a normal human, he was still not so far removed from the human condition that this sort of exertion would not exhaust him. It was a good reminder of his limits before hitting any further confrontations. He was not yet a god.

Most notable, though, was the effect his thousand hand ability had on his stamina and his mana. He had misjudged his mana consumption, and in doing so, he had lost his mana body ability. For now, the temporary loss of some of his boosted stats left him drained and weary, a fatigue he would never be used to. It was something that no amount of training could prepare a body for, and as for his body, it felt different in a way. Sick almost.

A mental projection of the ability popped up in his vision. It was a good time to check his progress with the ability, at least.

Notification: Thousand Handed - Current ability progress 7/1000

The ability had barely increased. He would just need to find a safer way to use it if this was the effect it had on him. He couldn't be paralyzed from stamina and mana fatigue every time he used an ability, just for the sake of trying to level it up.

Seraph stood, having at least regained enough stamina to move, and in doing so, he was able to catch his reflection in the glass window of the office. His face looked bruised, and his skin hung loosely, sagging off of his bones. His body was pale and emaciated, similar to those who had known extreme hunger. It was as if his body was forced to consume itself to match the energy output, and in a sense, his body had done exactly that. It had fed on itself when his energy reserves became exhausted.

For Seraph to be in such a situation was almost comical. He who had reached toward god-hood had actually run out of mana. It was laughable, but as he would always remember, not impossible. At least not currently. Until he was able to regain some of his former strength, he would need to be much more careful. Especially if he intended to use the thousand handed ability. Its use would require a delicate balance of precision and power, and that was something he was unsure he could manage in his current state.

For now, he resigned himself to limit its use. He would only use it if no other options remained—a trump card only to be utilized as a last resort due to its high mana burn that he could not simply maintain currently. The cost of using this ability in the absence of mana could easily render him unable to continue fighting.

Seraph watched the emaciated thing that was his reflection slowly return to normal as he regained his mana reserves. First the fullness returned to his cheeks and the color to his skin. His arms and legs regained some of their mass, and the little physique that he possessed returned.

When he finally felt that he was back to normal, he pulled his gaze away from his reflection, down to the body that lay crumpled lifelessly at his feet. He then looked toward his father. Paul's chest was rising and falling as a sign of life. Soon Erin's death would offer him yet another boon as he patted his new Cat's Claw and thought of the Starcall ability he had taken from her. When used correctly and without hesitation, it could easily decide any conflict.

It was not an ability that was meant to be wasted on the weak, and now Seraph had ensured it wouldn't be.

Within minutes, the lifeless body before him began to disappear as, little by little, it dissipated into the nothingness of whatever abyss this place was built upon. Consumed by the dungeon, Any physical evidence that Erin had ever existed in this place was erased forever. But it was what came after the erasure that Seraph waited for. He waited for the stat boost that always followed when one consumed another within the dungeon. He waited for a familiar jolt of power. He waited, but it never came.

"Figures," Seraph muttered with a curse as he looked at the undisturbed floor where Erin's body had lain. The dungeon restored everything to how it had been, and now all that could be seen was a thick layer of dust that suggested that no one had been here in years. When the familiar jolt of power never came, Seraph realized what that meant. Erin had been truly weak—even beyond the standards he had known for weakness. For him to not even gain a single stat point from her death meant that she had remained at the most basic level: level one. Level ones rarely offered any sort of bonus for their consumption. It was a check the dungeon had put into place to prevent predatory camping of new players at spawn and entry points.

Not that it had stopped him in the past. There were ways around it. The easiest of which was to power level the fresh faces who entered the dungeon and then consume them early. It was an easy and quick way to build up large stat gains. In his past life, Seraph had been almost killed that way.

A rare smile appeared on his face in memory of how things had been before, when he and his guild of player killers had rapidly gained strength beyond anything anyone else could ever compare with. A good memory that he dismissed before he came back to reality.

The reality was that once again he was

alone. His father lay only a few feet from him, slumped over and unconscious. Whatever partnership they might have been able to manage, it was clear it would never come to pass. Paul had been unable to separate his feelings as a father from the situation, and Seraph had been forced to act. Though as he watched Paul's chest rise and fall, he was still thankful the man was breathing. He had not intended to kill him, and he still wished for his father's survival.

He wished it enough, in fact, that he had left the required number of tokens out for him to move on to the next phase—an opportunity at continued survival that Seraph had rarely granted anyone. Though there was still something about the situation that lingered in his mind as wrong. Seraph thought for a minute and realized what it was.

Paul, his father, was still an obstacle in his way, and the last thing he needed was for Paul to ignore the tokens in his hand and go looking for him instead. Seraph was unsure of how much more this phase had to offer, but he was certain that the danger would only grow exponentially as he further explored and tried to find the dungeon seed. He refused to compromise his mission on the off-chance that his father would wake and either seek him out to rejoin as a party—his assistance at this point a hindrance

—or seek him out in search of vengeance or some other ill-conceived sense of duty.

The man was an obstacle, but Seraph couldn't bring himself to kill him. Even though the man was his father, Seraph couldn't figure out why he couldn't bring himself to do it, especially this early on when a few quick power boosts would help him to set up a new empire that would rival and eventually surpass anything he or his guild had achieved in that other lifetime. In spite of all that, there was still something that was missing, something that he needed to fix. Seraph stared at the unconscious man. He really didn't want to kill him, but he couldn't risk his goal being interrupted by this man demanding answers about where his new partner was either. Seraph's gaze lingered on the tokens he had placed near Paul's unconscious body, and the answer came to him. A way to remove his father without killing him.

Without further hesitation, Seraph reached out and grabbed the tokens he had laid down at Paul's side. He admonished himself for taking so long to come up with a solution to his current problem. He really should have thought of this before. In one single coherent motion, he placed all ten of the tokens into Paul's hand and forced the activation. Instantly, the man's unconscious body was sent on to the next phase, and for the moment at least, he was no longer Seraph's problem.

Seraph stared at the spot on the ground where Paul had been minutes previously. Slowly but surely, the dungeon reclaimed the spot as the dust disturbed by the man's presence returned, and in behavior not typical to him, Seraph spoke aloud, "Bye, Dad."

Without another thought, Seraph left the office to explore the rest of the school and try to find whatever other secrets it still had to offer.

CHAPTER 17: THE REMAINING

As he left the office, Seraph slid his forearm into the Cat's Claw to equip it. The weapon felt good on his arm as he adjusted the nylon straps for a tighter, closer fit. It was a good weapon. An extension of his own body, it was comfortable and deadly, and he would take very good care of it. He had once used something similar in his past life, and while it was not a weapon he had achieved legendary status with, he was certainly not unfamiliar. It would be well used in his hands.

The group had dwindled down to just him, and he felt good to be off on his own. In a sense, solo had always been his natural state. Without the need to hide who he really was, or what he was capable of, he felt complete confidence in his ability to take down any threat. Seraph was no longer obligated to try to tone down his abilities for the sake of others and had no need to hide himself. For now, at least, he was free.

Walking down the hall, he noticed the smell of dirt clinging to him. He looked behind him and saw the still-lingering clouds of dust that his heavy footsteps had kicked up. He laughed as he saw the trails he had made in the dirt, and as his laughs echoed down the halls, he felt nothing but excitement.

His blood rushing in eager anticipation, nothing quite compared to the feelings that adventuring alone brought up in him, feelings that made him feel alive and in control of himself. Seraph was free of the constraints of having to act a part that wasn't him, and though he was almost recklessly happy, he was still tuned into his surroundings. His altered senses revealed no current danger to be feared. This was his element.

He walked down the hall, looking at old pictures and trophies, photos of graduating classes in their multitudes. Seraph quickened his pace, and he caught sight of a classroom at the end of the row of awards. The sign above the door read 1A. With no additionally identifying information, Seraph moved to clean the dust and grime from the glass pan on the classroom door. He looked through and saw desks piled up, one on top of the other. Whatever this room had been, it hadn't been in use for a long time. This wasn't what he was looking for he was sure, so he turned around and continued to explore.

He didn't think it would be that easy, and not finding what he was looking for on the first try wasn't a surprise. He came to the second classroom—this one marked 1B. A name on the door read "Mr. Johnston." Finding a name plate was a good indicator that this classroom had been in use. Seraph tried to remove the grime and dirt from this window, but still he couldn't see inside. The interior of the window was covered in some sort of black residue.

Seraph was in a mood to fight, but he wasn't going to take any risks, so he used his new Starcall ability to summon the point of light on his side of the doorway centered in this air, and he let it charge for a few moments. As he waited, he checked his surroundings and noticed nothing amiss that he needed to be concerned about. Just yet, at least. He knew he wasn't alone, but he wasn't sure if he was alone in the halls. For now, nothing was nearby.

With a loud thud he knocked on the door three times, each knock louder than the last. He exerted enough force to dent the door and partially cave it in. He smiled at his handiwork and prepared himself to fight as he heard quick movements and scraping on the floor coming from the other side of the doorway. As if to confirm that something was there, the door shook as something hit it from the other side.

Perfect! thought Seraph as he grabbed the door handle and opened the door. He turned his back away from the doorway as he released the Starfall that he had been charging.

What appeared to have once been a man, stumbled out of the doorway in a frenzied state, screaming in incomprehensible guttural noises as it clutched at its eyes. It's skin was green and gangrenous, covered in thick boils that oozed puss. Its clothing was in relative disrepair, rotting at the seams and heavy with mold and mildew.

Ah, thought Seraph with a smile. *A Drowned One. That's interesting.* A Drowned One was a type of undead that usually, but not always, had a water-related death. However, they were most commonly known for their requirement of water nearby in their undeath. It was not a basic type of undead. Any attack, whether it landed or not, had a chance to apply a necrosis or gangrene—neither of which resolved itself out of battle. It was best to make this quick. With one quick motion, while the Drowned One was still unable to see him, Seraph thrust the Cat Claw up and forward while grabbing the top of the monster's skull by its slimy skin and the wispy tuft of hair it still possessed. The sharp knife-like points of the Cat's Claw easily cut through the rotted flesh, tissue, and bone.

Despite what should have been a death blow, the drowned man roared in anger as it swung its arms wildly, trying to kill the thing which had hurt it. This wasn't a problem for Seraph. As he pulled the blades of the Cat Claw out of the back of the monster's skull, he applied pressure in a downward curve, severing its spinal cord. The monster fell to the ground lifelessly for a true death.

As he pulled the blades out, thick white pus dripped to the ground, and his blades were a deep, reddish black from the coagulated blood with flecks of gray brain matter.

"That won't do" Seraph mumbled to himself as he bent over and wiped the claw's blades on the drowned one's rotted shirt, noticing as he did the name tag above the undead man's heart that read "Mr. Johnston."

With no signs of other monsters within the classroom, Seraph stepped forward, through the doorway of classroom 1B.

Scorch marks marred the walls in blackened angry scars. The few remaining desks were heavily burnt, their metal frames warped from exposure to extreme heat. The room was heavy with moisture and the smell of mildew. In the middle of the room pooled fetid, green water. Seraph cast a quick glance around the room, seeing if anything caught his eyes, and on the desk that had belonged to Mr. Johnston, he saw a set of keys that he was sure he would find useful.

Though Seraph did not see or hear anything that hinted at the presence of monsters, he was still wary of the standing pool of water in the room. A lesson he would always remember was that few things, inside the dungeon or outside, were ever really harmless.

Treat everything like a threat and be surprised by nothing. The pool of water was an unknown that he kept his eyes on, and as he walked toward the desks and grabbed the keys, he was then not surprised when the first rotted hand began to pull itself out of the water. Nor was he surprised when another set of hands followed swiftly after.

A normal adventurer might have been intimated or even scared at what appeared to be a spawning point right in the middle of the room he was in—effectively trapping him from escape —but Seraph was not normal by any means, and he knew what many adventurers did not—if this was a Drowned One spawning point, which Seraph was positive it was, it was limited to spawning a number equal to however many people had originally died in the room, and though the room was not small, Seraph still believed the number to be more than manageable.

Seraph put off grabbing the keys for now and ran toward the spawning pool, careful to avoid its edges. He would be a fool to forget that the dead hands of the drowned ones could still easily reach out and grab him if he was unwary, pulling him under to be torn apart. It was a grisly end, but one he could easily avoid.

Effortlessly, Seraph dispatched the Drowned One as it was still dragging itself out of the pool, He managed the same for the second, but by the time he was able to face the third, it had already pulled itself out from the pool to come after him, its arms stiff and outreached as it tried to kill him. It was not on the same level as the one with the name tag he had killed previously.

He dodged and weaved as more and more of the drowned ones emerged from the pool, careful to try to avoid exerting himself. Easy opponents or not, he was unsure how many he faced, and the last thing he needed was to be killed because of a fatigue debuff. As he moved, he struck where he could and cut and severed tissue and tendons alike. What he could not kill, he could maim, and within minutes, the drowned ones which had not been killed out-right by severing their spinal cord at least had their movements severely inhibited.

Seraph took his time to finish killing the rest. Though he was tired, he felt he had managed pretty well to keep from over doing it, and as he grabbed the keys in his hands, he took stock of how many of the things he had killed. Eleven in total. "Not bad at all."

Before heading off, he decided to put the experience he had just gained farming to work, putting the two stat points from the levels he had gained into endurance. This was a marathon and not a sprint. He would need an extra reserve to pull from—he was sure of that—and he needed to try and avoid having another spell of fatigue.

He counted a total of four keys, instantly dismissing what looked like a car key as being unimportant. He also dismissed the key marked 1B. He'd use it to lock the room behind him to make sure when the spawn reset nothing could approach him from behind. But, aside from that, it had no use, which left the remaining two keys

—one marked maintenance, and the other one wasn't marked at all.

An unmarked key was hardly a lead, which left him with the idea of searching for the maintenance room.

Name: Luca Fernandez
Race: Fallen
Aliases: None
Passives Abilities
Body of Mana

Abilities
Thousand Handed 34-1000
Starfall 6-1000
Level: 5 of 999

Unassigned Stat Points: 0
Current Experience: 3-90
STR: 2 **INT:** 1 **AGI:** 3
WIS: 1 **LCK:** 1 **PHY:** 0*
END: 4 **PER:** 3
SOL: $04240*

CHAPTER 18: REVELATIONS

Ragged breathing echoed down the hall; the empty lockers, rusted by age, further propelled the noise into the distance, acting as amplifiers to the sounds that Seraph made as he struggled to get his breathing back under control. Even with the extra points he had put into endurance to boost his stamina, it was still not enough to ward against his battle fatigue completely. Thankfully, the hallway was bereft of life except for him, and he saw no signs of monsters in various states of undeath haunting or roaming the halls.

Feeling somewhat safe—at least, as safe as the situation warranted—he allowed himself a moment of respite as he propped his back against one of the less rusted-looking lockers to catch his breath. The brief moment of relaxation was enough to coax his body into slowly regaining his strength. All the while he remained on guard for enemies and threats that might take their opportunity to fall upon him while his stamina was low.

His labored breathing grew less labored as the minutes passed until Seraph finally felt he had recovered enough of his stamina to continue. he was still trying to find the Dungeon Seed by searching the remaining portions of the school he had yet to explore, hoping to find whatever door or lock the key he had found belonged to.

Following his encounter in the classroom of Mr. Johnston, and his subsequent encounter with the Drowned Ones and the abuse of their spawn point, Seraph felt more physically ready to meet any challenge or enemy that might come his way than he had since his rebirth. But despite his readiness, he had no further notable encounters as he went room by room, clearing classroom and closet alike as he continued down the hall, working to exhaust all avenues of possibility for the location of the Dungeon Seed before continuing on.

Though no notable encounters occurred, he still came across several lower level monsters.

Within what had been a computer lab, he had been quick to strike down wights that had settled down among the rusted cables beneath the work desks. Though quick and easy to dispatch, the encounter with the wights had been a reminder that he was not alone. A reminder that he was still within the dungeon, and as such, he was always in danger. That mentality further reinforced his posture of awareness.

It was a posture that had saved him from catastrophe when he had gone to clear what he had originally thought was a janitor's closet. Seraph had been surprised to find a small teachers break area instead, filled with the rotting corpses of school staffers, milling around in their state of undeath—all of whom quickly descended upon him with reflexes beyond what a corpse should have.

As the bodies pressed into him and tried to tear into his flesh with tooth and claw, he was able to activate his Thousand Handed ability and used the spectral limbs to push the zombies off and away from him, putting much-needed distance between himself and the zombies. He then used this distance to eliminate them as he then had time to maneuver his way through the horde, destroying their brains and brain stems at leisure.

Nothing further occurred as he cleared

the rest of the rooms. Nothing elite crossed his path. Nothing beyond the most basic of monsters, and nothing that he could build real strength on or that would help him progress in his quest. Nothing that could even be viewed as irregular or something he had never encountered before. The rest of the rooms on the hallway cleared, his frustration with the situation grew. He had still not found the Dungeon Seed, nor had he found the maintenance room where he thought the seed was kept—the maintenance room he was sure the key he had found belonged to.

As he continued to explore, he finally found his forward progress inhibited by a set of closed double doors with reinforced glass panes that allowed him to see the other side. He caught a faint trail of dried blood, the brown rust-like substance heavily staining the floor but barely perceivable. Despite his low perception, he was still able to make out the trail.

Looking through the small windows on the door, he followed the trail with his eyes. The other side was as dusty and dirty as the rest of the school, but nothing stood out to him—except the trail leading deeper into the ever-widening common area. Where it went, he was unable to tell. His night vision heavily assisted him in the gloom, but it did not help much with his depth perception. He would need to follow the trail by foot, and his heart began to race in excited anticipation. As his strength continued to grow, so too did his need to test himself, and he had the impression he would soon be doing exactly that.

From what he could see through the small windows on the door, the other side was as dusty and decrepit as every other part of the school. It appeared to be empty, but Seraph knew better as he saw that trail of blood leading away into the darkness. He had already grown bored with the regular monsters on this side of the door, and he had a minor suspicion he had already killed every monster present. With a smile, he stepped forward and pushed through the doors, ready to continue his search.

He carefully followed the trail that led away from the hallway into the wider common area, snaking around the broken tables and stopping in front of a group of busted vending machines. The food that hadn't been taken had long since been reduced to dust, the wrappers faded beyond recognition. The trail led to a dead end, which left him with one option—head deeper into the dark. Within a few steps, the temperature in the room quickly dropped, and the air crackled with energy.

This is exactly what I've been looking for, he

thought as he noticed the obvious change in the environment.

Notification: Now Entering Phase 3. If you would like to skip ahead and go directly to Hometown, please select 'yes'. NOTE - Caution, all deaths within Phase 3 and beyond are permanent.

Would you like to skip ahead? Yes/No?

Well, this is interesting, he thought. *I had thought all the deaths were permanent from the beginning and that I had sent the others directly into Phase III, but if this where I am, and this is actually Phase III, then the others must already be in Hometown.* Seraph wasn't surprised by this. It was a usual trick of dungeons to reward those who dared to do more, and for those who took the easy way out, and quit in advance, they were never given the offer or opportunity of achieving greater power.

The screen disappeared as he mentally selected "No." He had no intention of missing out on a chance to grow stronger—regardless of the risk to him. He hadn't come this far to quit already. Not when every step put him closer to his goal.

"Cousin!" shouted a raspy voice from the center of the room, far into the dark. "Come here, cousin. I can smell the scent of the damned on you. come here; it has been so long since I've had a guest."

Seraph recognized the voice, even in this altered state. This was Reverend. He stepped forward as asked, and as he crossed the threshold, more was revealed as he saw what remained of the guests the voice was referencing, their mutilated bodies nailed to the wall at the far edge of the room.

In the center of the room, propped up—his body somehow attached to a jagged piece of earth that had thrust up through the floor—was Reverend. Or at least it was something that used to be Reverend, for the withered monstrosity that Seraph saw before him could hardly be called a man—even though the monstrosity closely resembled the man he had once known.

This is not the man I knew, he thought. Gone was the mane of black hair that Reverend had been so proud of. Instead, in its absence hung white and gray hair, thin, wispy, and wild. The man's eyes no longer shined through with strength, the passion of his convictions, or even his resilience. Instead, all Seraph could see was empty eye sockets burned black where those pale orbs had been burned out.

Whatever had happened here, Seraph promised to end it now. He could not allow Reverend to live such a cursed existence, and as he promised to end it, he stepped forward.

"Good, cousin. Good. Come closer. What is your name?" asked Reverend.

If what he had read in the Wormwood Report was correct, he knew Reverend likely bore some resentment toward him, and to the guild. Now was not the time to reveal himself, but with his low charisma and luck stats, he also knew he couldn't get away with a lie. However, he could get away with a half-truth.

"Announce yourself!" demanded the withered figure of Reverend impatiently as it turned its head, its empty eye sockets facing Seraph. "Who are you?"

"My name is Luca and I'm a new adventurer. Tell me, cousin, how are we related? What is your name?" Seraph asked.

The withered figure cackled in a mad laugh. "You lie, cousin, there are no new adventurers—Lord Seraph killed them all. Just as he has killed this world. I was known as Reverend, though now I am little more than a shade, a persistent shadow of darkness in this place, cousin. Like you, I am a type of demon. I once served the great genocide himself—the Black Seraph. I served him, and I served his guild of murderers for many years, until I came to this place and served the children as their protector. There were twenty-eight in all. Twenty-eight children that I saved when the Wormwood spread this far."

Seraph thought he knew enough about where this was heading to ask the right follow-up questions. "What is Wormwood, and do you know what those things are outside? Are they related? And how did you manage to save the children?"

Reverend drew a quick breath and sniffed the air. "It's bad luck to talk about those things.

They are not monsters. They are an end, and even within the dungeon, they can find ways inside. It is best to ignore them and continue living."

But on the next question his demeanor changed. "Of course, they are related. This is my life's work. Wormwood is the celestial poison manifested on Earth to rid it of humanity, to rid the cosmos itself of all life.

As for the children? Well, they escaped into the dungeon. I implanted myself with a Dungeon Seed, and from my mana and my body I helped it grow. Through me they escaped—to Hometown —and I remained, stuck forever. Embedded into the portal."

Seraph responded with as much support as he could muster. "That's terrible, Reverend. Is there anything I can do to help?"

If Reverend heard him, he didn't respond.

Seraph needed to know more. He needed to know what Reverend would tell others who made it this far. "Who is this Black Seraph, and how do we defeat him?"

Those dead eyes narrowed, and somehow Reverend shifted his body to close the distance between him and Seraph. "Cousin, you don't know of the Black Seraph? Be warned then and be wary. With his appetite for power, he has consumed millions. Millions more he has doomed to death or killed outright. He is a monster to be stopped at all costs, yet I do not know how to stop him. Though he calls himself Black, he is neither a creature of bane or of bone, nor is aligned with the holy. He holds his allegiances elsewhere and to no one. He is doom, and his is blight."

Reverend moved his body back onto its pedestal and began to mutter to himself. However, he muttered loudly enough for Seraph to hear the ramblings of a madman. "How could he not know? Who doesn't know? Of course, he knows. Of course, he doesn't know. Yes, he should. No, he shouldn't." The internal deliberation continued until Reverend's eyes lit up— one side lighting up with purple flame, the other with blue flame. Both eyes then turned to him, each side seemingly independent of the other. He asked, "Cousin, what year is it? Yes, cousin, what year is it?" Reverend spoke in mocking contempt.

Seraph was unsure how to proceed, but fate interfered. The double doors of the hallway shut behind him, and the sound of the doors locking announcing that he was stuck. Something was coming his way. An audible click announced that he was committed. There would be no retreating from this.

CHAPTER 19:
THE WEBS
WE WEAVE

Twin eyes glared at him, eyes of fire, and eyes of the abyss, one purple and one blue. Each eye represented a different aspect of the Reverend's state of undead, and each eye asked the same lingering question. They looked impatient, hungry for Seraph to stall, looking for a reason to satisfy an urge not for flesh alone, but for the kill.

Seraph looked into those eyes, wondering just what kind of monster Reverend had become. He thought perhaps it was either some kind of Lord-Caliber Wright or a Darkness Caller—a type of spirit trapped to a place that drew others in to share in its misery. Seeing the duel colors of purple and blue, Seraph thought perhaps maybe Reverend was some sort of combination of both.

"Did he not hear?" Reverend mumbled to

himself as his monstrous body began to quiver, ready to move and strike. The bodies of the other guests hanging from the walls were a clear reminder of what Reverend was now capable of.

"First, will you tell me what happened here? How did you end up this way?" Seraph asked, buying time. "I would like to hear your story."

The monster's eyes glowed red in anger. Reverend then sighed, the anger extinguished, and with that its orbs returned to their usual colors. "Fine, but only because it has been such a long time since I spoke with anyone but ourselves."

"Thank you," Seraph replied as respectfully as he could manage. He knew that whatever had happened to Reverend was, at least, partially his fault. He needed to fix this—not out of some sense of right and wrong, or some sense of justice, but because Reverend had once been an ally and as close to a friend as Seraph had got.

Reverend moved his rotted arms to stroke his face in contemplation. *No,* thought Seraph, *not rotted at all. The black plate mail he wore in life appears to have melded with this new body of his."*

Reverend suddenly stopped stroking his face as both eyes turned blue. He drew in a deep breath. It was a breath that rattled against bones and deep fibers. A breath that Seraph was unsure even drew air.

It took the undead a minute, as if this was his first time in years he had heard his own voice. When he spoke, it was deep and serious with none of the chaotic vestiges he had shown earlier. To Seraph's eyes, it appeared that some minor changes had occurred as well as more of the man and less of the monster was brought forth.

"I failed, you see," he explained. "I came here to find a way to prevent the spread of the green mist, the miasma outside—or what I termed Wormwood. I left most of those details in my old office. If you find it, bring it here and I will unseal it and share it with you, imparting the knowledge of how to access artifacts of my old guild—Carrion Crow. That will conclude Phase III and my responsibilities to Amarath."

Seraph nodded his head in understanding, not wanting the monster to know he already had found the report and that it was on his person. Even a low luck stat could pay dividends.

"But how did you get here?" Seraph asked as he probed for information. The monster was friendly, for now, but in the dungeon there were no guarantees. "And become this... well, I'm not quite sure what you are, I'm sorry to say."

"Brazen aren't you, cousin?" chided Reverend with the mocking laughter of the dead. "When the Wormwood Phenomenon began to spread this way, it did so at a speed we had never seen before. Usually, we tried to evacuate well in advance, but this time it wasn't possible.

I tried to buy time for my children to evacuate into the dungeon using the seed I had planted, and though I stopped the Fetchers—the monsters that can leave the green mist and look for victims—it was still not enough time for the Dungeon Seed to sufficiently mature."

"What's a Fetcher?" asked Seraph curiously wanting to confirm it was the same thing from his memory." Despite how it may have seemed, Seraph had had limited contact with the Miasma and its monsters until after he had secured his Dark Mantle ability, an ability which afforded him massive defensive boosts to both raw stats and status protection.

"You wouldn't have any need to know of

it," explained Reverend with a satisfied look on his face. "The Fetchers are wretched things. They are small and deformed, but they are quick too, with eyes in all directions. Much stronger than you would guess for their stature, they collect many of the people who are to be left behind, and they take them somewhere else—I'm not sure where. You'll find out either in person, or when you fetch my report. As you make discoveries, you'll find it automatically updates to reflect new topics."

This was impressive information. He regretted not having access to it in his previous life. "I didn't know that," he admitted with an appreciative nod. "But what are you now? What happened next?"

"One thing at a time, cousin," responded Reverend, the blue in one eye beginning to move deeper into purple. "The Dungeon Seed wasn't done, you see. It still needed something else to grow and mature, and I offered the only thing I could find—the people who were with me. I'm sure you may have encountered some of them— reanimated, soulless, intelligent things that they are now. But in the end, the sacrifices I made were still insufficient. So, I offered myself instead and took the immature Dungeon Seed. I cut deep into my own chest and gave myself to nurture it.

"The result," continued Reverend, "is what you see here. The children were allowed to evacuate to Hometown, and I was bound to this location, forever unable to leave. The dungeon has made of me a Wright, though my captivity has made of me something darker and fouler still. Something that is both me, and of me, and separate from me. A thing that claws in the dark.

"So, now I find myself repeating questions I should never have to repeat," said Reverend, his voice tinged with anger and some regret as the vestiges of the man began to fade as the purple orb flared again. "Tell me, what year is it? For how long, dear cousin, have I been trapped here?"

Seraph considered his answers carefully. Based on what he had seen and heard so far, this portion of the dungeon appeared to have continued to exist within the future that Seraph was from, but it also existed within the present.

"Careful, cousin," interrupted the abomination that was Reverend. "I can smell a lie, and you reek of falsehoods."

"I don't know for how long you've been trapped here. I'm also not entirely sure where this is. But I can tell you the year. It's 2010," answered Seraph without trying to give away many other details.

"Impossible!" shouted Reverend as both eyes blazed with light. "I have been here, trapped, for endless decades, alone in the dark as everyone I ever cared about and knew has fallen or been consumed. It has been decades, adventurer! Cousin, you lie."

"I promise you, I haven't lied!" shouted Seraph as the floor began to break under Reverend's body, and things begin to shift out of sight, revealing what had been hidden. Seraph had thought Reverend was stuck to a pillar, but what he had thought was a pillar appeared to be a great black root, gangrenous and vile-looking. It appeared to have grown from the man's torso and embedded itself into the ground.

The floor continued to break as Reverend sped forward like a serpent, the wooden planks underneath him parting like a wave, reforming behind him. The bulk of his body was far greater than anything Seraph had guessed, and now he witnessed some of what lay beneath the floor.

The Reverend Seraph had been speaking to was little more than a puppet for the abomination that had been lurking beneath the floor. Hiding the true body of the monster that lived below his feet.

Still, the monster came at him with a

speed that Seraph had difficulty keeping up with, and as he went to a guard position with his Cat's Claw, he wondered for a brief second if it was even possible to get out of this situation.

Without warning, and before Seraph could see anything, Reverend was upon him, hands like claws upon his throat, and duel orbs of purple looking directly into his eyes. The monster sniffed once, then twice. "You lie, cousin."

As Seraph went to protest, he was thrown across the room with enough force that when he hit the ground he heard an audible snap. His off-arm was broken on impact. Instant pain flooded through Seraph's mind, but he couldn't think about the pain, regardless of its distraction.

He needed to walk away from this alive. He grabbed the pills he had found earlier from within his pocket, taking two of them to numb the pain as he tried to assess the situation. Reverend sped across the room again to finish the job and kill him as Seraph began to mentally charge his Starcall ability—this time, focusing the point on himself.

Seraph's vision wasn't working like it should have been—a sign of damage to his body that he didn't want to consider. He never saw

Reverend as he was lifted off the ground again, this time the monster laughing as he was struck across the face with a blow that split his cheek on the sharpened high bones of his skull. As he spat out white flakes in bloody spittle, he wondered about deeper damage until he realized he had just lost teeth.

Coughing up blood, he knew if this lasted any longer he was likely going to die. This was too early to face alone. This monster that Reverend had become was far beyond him. Once again, his ego and over-confidence would be his undoing.

"Weak. Pathetic," muttered Reverend with regard to Seraph. "Maybe he wasn't lying about being a new adventurer. Only new adventurers and regular humans are this weak. No, no; can't be. He lies! He lies!" Eyes flashed in disagreement, but the monster continued to move across the room where it had thrown Seraph.

An idea came to Seraph as he struggled to remain consciousness. His ears rang, and the sensation of vertigo hit him. He just needed to present the Wormwood Report, and the dungeon would be forced to send him onward to safety. Seraph held no illusion that whatever Reverend had become, this would not be the day that Seraph freed him.

"Stop!" yelled Seraph as he released his Starcall, the room turning to white as he was unable to turn away in time. It seemed to work though, as the blow that Seraph thought would kill him never came. He quickly used the time to reach out into his spacial pocket and pull out the Wormwood Report. "I have the Wormwood Report, Reverend. Stop this madness."

The monster stopped, and though its eyes had not been affected like Seraph's had, they still lingered with some vestiges of limitation. "Let me see that, cousin. If you've lied again, I'll spend the rest of your life flaying your skin and tissue from your bones, reanimating and healing you only to repeat the process."

Seraph blindly held the report out, and the undead man quickly snatched it out of his hands.

"This report has been activated already, not just found," accused Reverend, its eyes flashing deep red and purple. "You're one of us, aren't you? You're of Carrion Crow? What of the guild? How do they fare? Only officers are taught how to undo the seal."

The monster looked on in wonder, and

Seraph took the time to stand up and at least try to get his posture correct. He leaned in to whisper into the monster's ear. "You once called me Lord. I who was the Black Seraph. This truly is a new beginning. Be well until I come for you again".

The monster looked back in confusion and reverence at the revelation as Seraph disappeared.

The dungeon had accepted his quest completion.

CHAPTER 20: WELCOME TO HOMETOWN

Gradually, Seraph began to wake, his face pressed into the fibers of the office carpeting he had been passed out on. His head was heavily swollen and itching from the rough fabric. Impulsively, he went to scratch his face and was met with an immediate response of agony as pain wracked his whole body. Sensation was returning to his limbs, and consciousness returned to his mind. The idle sensation of carelessness he had been experiencing disappeared as he was reminded of the events that had put him where he was.

Badly hurt and near death, Seraph had barely been able to escape being killed at the hands of his old guild member and companion,

Reverend. He had become an abominable type of undead wright, a Dweller in the Dark.

At heart, Seraph knew he had been outclassed by the monster as he had been unable to do anything to stop him. Until his injuries finished healing, he had to resist the compulsive need to check his gum line to see if he was still missing his teeth, or if they had regrown already.

What Seraph knew was that he hadn't been unconscious for long. That he was currently starting to feel pain meant that the pills he had taken were wearing off, but not enough time had passed yet for the dungeon to heal his injuries. At least, not all of them. He no longer felt the jagged tears in his chest and labored breathing indicative of a collapsed lung or broken ribs. Those, at least, had healed.

Trying to stand, he found the pain was still too intense, and he had to calm himself to wait it out on the floor. Then a hand grabbed him by the back of his head and sharply pulled him off the floor, a light flashing in front of his eyes. Behind that light, he could only guess at who or rather what was examining him.

Anger and the force of wrath filled his body as his stature adjusted itself in the wake of his temporarily boosted status.

"Let go of me!" Seraph demanded with a voice full of hostility as he attempted to interject a hint of his power into the demand. He did this despite knowing it would do no good. Seraph could hear the fatigue in his own voice.

"He's still alive!" shouted a voice that Seraph knew he recognized from somewhere. "Go ahead and let the higher ups know he's going to make it." Whatever the man had been looking for, he had found it, because as soon as he picked Seraph up, he was placing him down on the ground.

Seraph strained to try to look at the man who had grabbed him, but his eyes had still not adjusted, and for his effort to look, his only response was one of pain.

"Hey, listen kid, knock that off. Just give it a few more minutes, so the healing can kick in and take care of you. You look like absolute shit, I'm sorry to say, and that face of yours has taken one hell of a beating. I guess that's just what to expect from a guy who just graduated first in his tutorial class. Congratulations, by the way," said the man.

"I'm Garen, and I've just got to say well done, kid. Well done. None of us on this side of the fence expected you to manage any of that on your own. I was positive you were a dead man walking until just now. Man, that was intense. Well done. Seriously. So, take a second to catch your breath and get your bearings. I'm going to unseal the other participants in a minute. Each of them has been sealed away in a sort of stasis, waiting for the tutorial class to end. We've just been waiting on you."

Notification: Quest Completed - Complete Phase III by presenting the Wormwood Report to the monster known as Reverend

Reward: 300 Sol, 150 Experience Points.

Reward: Gain a tailored ability.

Notification: Ability unlocked. "Cold Hands" At will, the user may siphon thermal energy on touch. The speed of the siphon is 3% per second, with an additional 1% per point in

Intelligence.

Notification: As the first person to complete Phase III, you have been granted an additional 300 Sol and an additional 150 experience points. Additionally, you have been granted two stat points to assign.

Notification: The Wormwood Report has been upgraded and transformed into the Wormwood Codex. Data on the Fetches and the Infernals has been added.

"Good," said Garen. "It seems like you're coming around—judging by that look in your eye that says you're reading status prompt notifications. Wait to assign any points till after this is done, okay?"

Garen looked down at Seraph, who was still lying on the ground. "Okay, give me a minute. This is really starting to bother me, kid." Garen bent down, his knees cracking with age, and reached out his hand to help Seraph up. Seraph, while prideful, accepted the help.

This wasn't a man he wanted to offend, and he was still feeling the sheer magnitude of the extent of his injuries. If he had been a normal man, he would likely be dead on the floor, or worse—back in that room with Reverend, still screaming as his skin got flayed. One of the benefits of the dungeon was that he could at least rule out permanent damage.

"Here," Garen said as he guided Seraph to a chair. As Seraph's vision began to clear, he saw that he had been seated at a table in what appeared to be a conference or training room. It was not lost on him that he was sitting alone.

Garen clapped his hands twice, and those who had been in stasis appeared—disheveled and confused. They then took seats in the other chairs around the table. Seraph inwardly cringed. This was not a confrontation that he wanted —this was just a side show he'd rather avoid. He looked around, and the others in the room avoided his eyes—at least, those who knew him. He was already a pariah. A suspicion confirmed when not even Paul would look his way.

Garen moved to the front of the conference room and began to speak. "For those of you who didn't hear me before, my name is Garen, and I handle in-processing into Hometown. I've some other duties and functions that go along with that, but you'll find out later about those. They aren't relevant to what we are doing right now. Let's focus on the fight and the hell you've all just been through. I hope you learned a lot because it only gets worse and deadlier from here. In spite of what you might think, this was done for your benefit.

"So..." Garen continued, looking at the group as he rubbed his hands together, "for those of you who are unfamiliar with this process, it's called an after action review—or a debriefing if you prefer? This is a convenient way to process and go through what it is that you've done, what it is that you've been through, and what you can do better.

I try to follow the three up and three down formula, but I'm not married to it. It just depends on the flow. That means focusing on ways to improve and sustain the good that you did, if anyone was wondering? First, let's focus on those participants among you who managed to be killed before the start of Phase III and were afforded a respawn."

"For the record, folks," Garen empathized for clarity, "we don't do second chances around here. If you die from here on out, it's for keeps."

From the back of the room, Alexander spoke up and asked, "Why wouldn't you just tell us that we would respawn if we died? I was terrified, and I know I wasn't the only one. That's not cool, man."

Seraph saw that most of the heads in the room nodded in agreement. *Fools. They're hardly able to realize the favor that's been granted to them,* Seraph thought in judgment.

"It's simple, it really is, and I'm guessing most of you," Garen answered as he looked at the group, his eyes lingering on Seraph for a moment, "aren't going to like the answer. You, all of you, are being cultivated to fight and to kill, but most of you are soft. These concepts are as foreign to you as hunger to a man that's never missed a meal. We needed you to learn and to overcome. Again, I repeat myself, this was done for your benefit most of all."

A clamor broke out among the participants as they yelled and screamed over each other, wondering what was going on. They screamed accusations at Garen, demanding to talk to whoever it was that Garen identified in his "*we*" statement. Garen held up his hands, asking for patience and silence, but all of them ignored the commands.

All but Seraph, who finally placed where he knew the man from. This man whom in that other life had been an early rival for Seraph. This man who was not a man at all. Garen was the leader of the elves who ruled over Hometown, and he answered directly to the spirit of the dungeon. He was not a man to be ignored or trifled with.

"Quiet. Quiet, please," repeated Garen, his face strained with the polite and practiced smile of a politician. When this still did not give him the attention he asked for, he used his power to demand it as he thrust a fist out and a wave of yellow energy forced the arguing participants back into their seats. A follow-up red wave silenced every sound from within the room except for him. People continued to yell, but no sounds could be heard.

Garen looked out at the shocked faces and shrugged, their discomfort wasn't his problem, and they had interrupted him. "Now, as I was saying—and, please in the future, do not make me repeat myself. I will not be as accommodating—we will be focusing first on those of you who died. Mary Anne, it was an interesting choice to go with the mermaid cosmetics.

We did try to work out the details for you after, but you refused our help. I hope the experience of suffocating out of water wasn't too traumatic. I imagine it was a bit awkward to die like that. It certainly looked unpleasant."

Seraph looked at the woman that Garen was talking to. Her face had gone from blushing in embarrassment to pale from the reminder.

"That said, I've taken some executive liberties and removed those cosmetic selections. This is why you're reverted to your human form. You'll be allowed to choose from a pre-set list of approved races, if you find your human form unappealing," he explained.

Mary Anne raised her hand, and Garen smiled, waving his hand to suspend and bypass the spell of silence he had cast. "What are the selections?" she asked. "I think I'd like to be an elf like you—and like the others, if that's okay?"

"Yeah, that's not going to happen," Garen replied. "I don't let anyone change their race to an elf. If you didn't choose it from the very beginning, that's on you. That's your mistake.

The elves will never be a selection on the pre-approved list—only the lesser races like humans, dwarfs, goblins, lizard men and the undead are on there."

"Could I have a little more information about these choices before making a decision?" she asked

Garen laughed at her. "That's on you to figure out. Just be more discerning with your choices from now on. They have actual consequences.

Speaking of consequences, I'm assigning you an adventurer rank of F for your performance in this tutorial. You'll receive a debt fine of 50 Sol, which is our currency, and a debt fine of 50 experience. Best of luck in your future battles."

Before she could protest or ask another question, Garen raised his hand, and the same light flashed again, and whatever sound she had wanted to make was gone.

Garen turned away from the woman and turned to the monstrous-looking man with bull horns at the table next to her and started speaking. "Next up we have Dwight. Now, Dwight, I really liked your cosmetic selection. A Minotaur can boost any team it's on, but you need to understand that until you upgrade your abilities and your gear you can't just absorb hits. A tank without armor is worthless.

I imagine it was quite the unpleasant sensation when Sadie's sword cut through your flesh like butter, leaving you gutted and bleeding out on the ground. You need to remember that a little healthy fear goes a long way toward self-preservation. Even though you made it past the starting point, I'm also granting you an adventurers' rank of F for your performance. You are also fined a debt of 50 Sol and 50 experience."

Next, Garen turned to the elven male behind Dwight—his ears a giveaway for what his cosmetic selections had been. "George, I know that being an elf brings with it feelings of elation that are difficult to control, but don't ever forget that the people who are here in the dungeon —now elf and human alike—are people that are masters of their craft and masters of the martial art that they specialize in."

"You can't just pick up a sword and be an expert. Especially, not trying to dual wield swords. You have to learn to crawl before you can walk. For your efforts, I'll be awarding you an adventurers' rank of C.

The willingness to close with an opponent is the true heart of the Warrior. When we're done here, you can have access to up to 5 training sessions with some elven trainers, myself included. I have no intention of wasting your raw talent and passion just because you've been reckless." Garen nodded at him and moved on.

"Alright, Jack," Garen said. "Jack, I'd like to commend you for being able to take advantage of the situation like you did. This was a difficult challenge for you—your abilities were not well-suited for the task—but through conniving and working with others, you were able to survive and actually get the award for being the first to collect the ten tokens. For these reasons, I'm awarding you an A rank as an adventurer.

Unfortunately, we do not currently have any necromantic trainers, so I cannot offer you that. As an award instead, I can offer one elite cosmetic selection that has a chance to change your racial attributions."

Garen turned and looked toward Alexander. "Alexander, you did your job as expected, but nothing you did stood out. You are neither an expert nor have any natural talent, but you were willing to close with the enemy, and that is the heart of the Warrior.

However, you also attempted to steal the

artifact off one of your party, and in doing so, you managed to be defeated. This is both shameful and embarrassing. For this reason, I'm assigning you an adventurer rank of D, and I will offer you two free training sessions with the spear.

Seraph knew who would come next, and he refused to look to see.

"Paul," Garen said. "I watched your progress with great interest. That you already had natural talent and training with a knife was evident, but I was impressed more so that you remained cool and collected during your fight with the Gigas.
These aspects impressed us. Less impressive was the distraction your female companion was for you.

For this reason, I am assigning you an adventurer rank of B. As a reward for your efforts, we are granting you an unbreakable knife that can extend up to four feet. We feel you will make good use of it."

Garen nodded at Paul and then moved on to an empty table. "The woman who was among you did not respawn," explained Garen. "When the soul and the spirit is destroyed, there's nothing left to come back. For those of you who knew her, apologies for your loss."

At last, Garen stood before Seraph. "You and I have already talked about your performance. We can talk further still, in private, about ways to improve. But for your efforts and for your results I deem you an A-ranked adventurer. The keys you found opened the door to the outside. Though Reverend was beyond you, he was not beyond the Infernals. In this way, you could have defeated him. Because you did not realize this course of action, I cannot grant you an S ranking.

Additionally, you were unable to recover the dungeon seed. For this reason, I also cannot grant you an S ranking. Also, like in the case of Jack, we do not have any trainers available that I believe will benefit you. In their absence, you will also be granted an additional elite cosmetic selection, if you so wish."

Garen walked back to the front of the room and snapped his fingers. "Alright, most of you are dismissed."

In an instant, only Paul, Seraph, Jack, and Alexander remained. The tension between them all was heavy and palpable. Seraph stared while the other three avoided his gaze.

"As the only survivors of the tutorial, and the first ones to go through it, you have a choice to make," explained Garen.

"The tutorial you were afforded is not free. There is a cost associated with it. To maintain the tutorial indefinitely for all future adventurers we would need to implement a tax on roughly 10% of all experience earned.

That 10% allows us to manage this tutorial, and it gives you humans a better chance at survival. Alternatively, we can use that 10% tax to give you more power now and put that debt on the remainder of humanity to pay back. Whatever you four decide, it needs to be a complete 100% vote in favor or against. Any questions?"

A hand was raised. Alexander's hand. "Do we get anything from other people in return for keeping the tutorial running? Or are we expected to live off gratitude? How would you power us up, and why would I want to give that up?"

Garen answered, "Those of you who hold a legendary class emblem will have it unlocked. Those of you who don't will be granted an elite class instead."

Seraph understood some of that sentiment as he thought of the Emblem that sealed away his power. The desire to be whole again was tempting. Seraph looked at the other two men and then to his father. His father turned away, unable to look at him.

"I also have a question," Seraph said. "How does the tutorial benefit humanity?"

Garen looked at Seraph in apparent appreciation for the question. "A good question. If the tutorial respawn was not in place, half of the participants of the tutorial would have died. I cannot say if all will have the same results, but it certainly will save lives. Everyone who goes through the tutorial will be stronger for it when they enter the actual dungeon."

"Garen?" asked Seraph, "I'd like to discuss with the other three humans this policy you want us to adopt. It should be quick. I just want to make the best call."

"Yeah, that's fine," responded Garen. "This is a big decision that is going to affect a lot more than just you. It's not something you need to rush through. Just remember that whatever you decide, that decision has to be unanimous.

The four humans grouped up to talk as Garen looked on.

"There's nothing to talk about." Alexander said. "I'm not going to pay a tax forever for a benefit I don't use, just for the sake of people I don't know. I was pathetic out there, but if I get a boost, I could become like a god. And I think Jack is with me on that from the way he's nodding his head. This isn't worth turning down elite and legendary class upgrades."

"Alright then," acknowledged Seraph. "What about your thoughts, Dad? Where do you fall with this?"

"You don't want to know my thoughts," Paul said darkly. "But this is bigger than my feelings. When I served in the Army, I learned there is a lot more to being a hero than just being strong. Integrity, courage, service, they all matter, but sometimes you have to be prepared to do the hard thing when life gives you no other option than to spit on your hands and hoist the black sails. I'll defer to whatever the group decides to make things easier.

Seraph nodded, appreciative of the blunt advice. He knew he would need to talk to Paul later. "Alright, Alexander, do you mind telling Garen then that we've made our decision?"

"Yeah, not a problem. I don't want any trouble, you know. This is just the best decision for me," he replied.

"Yes, I do know how it is," muttered Seraph

in disappointment.

Alexander turned to walk away, and Seraph tightened his grip on the Cat Claw that he always carried attached to his arm.

With a quickness that no one expected, he thrust the weapon through Alexander's skull, killing him instantly as blood and brain matter splattered from the force of the thrust. Alexander dropped dead to the floor, and the body began convulsing.

Seraph approached Garen, daring the other two men to disagree with him. "We accept the tutorial tax of 10% of all future experience to be imposed on us and all future humans who enter the dungeon."

"Great! I knew you had it in you," replied Garen with a smile. "And welcome to Hometown. The journey of a lifetime starts here."

You Have The Power Rate&Review

Please review the books you're reading when done. Especially if you like them. Not just for me, but for all authors you want to keep writing. Your reviews and how you review have a direct and immediate impact on our livelihoods. I make just enough off of these books to pay to write the next. Here is how reviews work on Amazon.

5 ⭐This was a good/great read.

This is the only rating that pushes authors towards more exposure because of the messed-up way Amazon ratings work, as I'll explain below.

4 ⭐This was acceptable/mostly good.

This is still counted as a positive review, but being below a 4.5 average reduces a book's discoverability. Once a book dips below a 4.5 average, Amazon stars to censor it. This is a soft negative as it's below that 4.5 threshold.

3 ⭐Needs Improvement/Bad/DNF

This is outright considered a negative review by

Amazon. Below a 4 star average, authors can't even PAY to run ads for their books.

2 ☆ This was awful

It takes two 5s to get back to a 4 average. I DNF because of how badly written the content was or how bad the editing was.

1 ☆ This person should not ever be allowed to write a book again. This is no different than storming into a manager's office and demanding a clerk or waitstaff, etc be fired.

Unfortunately, it takes five, five-star reviews to offset the damage of a single 1-star review to get back passed that 4.5 threshold.

For most books, a single 1-star review during launch will kill a book.

So be careful how you rate, and be sure to rate. This is a call to action in general for any author, not just for my books. Anything less than a 4 is a vote against an author saying stop writing. I don't believe it should be this way, but unfortunately, Amazon does.

Make sure to follow my author profile for new releases in the Pandemonium Universe
https://geni.us/BuyMyBooks
Thanks.

Make sure to follow my author profile for new releases and to check out other books.

https://geni.us/BuyMyBooks
Thanks.

Also included is a short sample chapter of an upcoming story, "Arcane Summoner"

ARCANE
SUMMONER
"PREVIEW"

CHAPTER ONE: ENTER ARCADIA. THE ANCIENT CITY

Like the rest of the world, Arcadia had grown silent. The ancient ruins stood open to all, but everyone living knew to stay away. It was just the way of things since the Sundering. The old cities were home to the Draugr and other monsters of the dark.

Zander knew this and went anyway. He was desperate and had been for a couple of weeks now and had grown tired of carefully trying to etch out a little bit of survival in his village. He was not alone. Rocktooth, his personal summon and guardian, stood by him. A golem towering over him, its face and hands were smooth.

Rocktooth looked down at him, and though the golem couldn't talk, Zander knew exactly what it was trying to say. *This is dangerous for you, do not do this.* He ignored the golem's concern and looked up at the sun to try for an accurate guess of how much daylight was left. *Little past midday. Four hours maybe.* He could get in and out before dark, but the Draugr in the buildings would still be a problem. They were far more active regardless of the time of day.

Through their connection, Zander could feel the quiet alarm and anxiety building up in his summons's subconscious. It was not a natural state for one of its kind to lead their master into avoidable danger. Together they walked as silently as they could on the crumbling grey stone path, stained in parts green from the overgrowth on the building, and darker still in others. The thought made him shudder.

Today they would be going deeper, where few if any scavenger parties had managed to breakthrough. *If I'm going to put myself in danger, I at least need to be smart about it.* He hoped to find something mostly untouched. Eventually, they arrived at the entrance to the Harrow they would be exploring, much of the paint had worn off with time, but part of the title could still be read in the ancient language. "hnologies".

Notification: Now Entering "The Ancient Ruins – Harrow"
Details: In ages past, humans used to assemble and work in places like these. Now, all that remains of their civilization are the monsters that dwell within these haunted burrows.

The building was old but sturdy with none of the wear or rot he'd seen in some of the other Harrows. He passed through the opening into what had once been a lobby. Half-melted plastic tables and furniture warped from time were thrown about as if something had been in a rage.

"C'mon, let's go," He said with a whisper as he poked at the magical core in the middle of the golem's torso with his staff. The golem's eyes lit up in response, reaffirming the contract between master and summon. "Follow me." To fit into the building, the golem started to shrink until he stood no bigger than a man. The magic was simple enough, but He needed more. He needed to learn. He needed a real teacher and that all led back to the sum of most of his problems. *Money. But at least today I might be able to find something worth trading.*

Zander waited before moving, stopping to listen, hoping he wouldn't hear the patter of feet that let him know Draugr was coming. *We're good.* He nodded at Rocktooth as he tried to open the rusted door to the stairway. He once learned the hard way that the ancient's had relied on another manner to move about their buildings. The door didn't budge.

He looked over at the door and imparted a message to Rocktooth. The golem's eyes flashed green, and Zander smiled cautiously. *Here goes.* He stepped back, and the golem walked to the steel door. The golem sent a flurry of messages to Zander's mind, and he stifled a laugh. The golem turned to Zander, and when He nodded, it placed a heavy stone hand on the door and pushed it forward. The door, rusted from age, was torn off of its hinges and fell to the ground, making far too much noise. Zander expected the Draugr or worse monsters to swarm the area immediately but heard nothing. *Maybe we'll be ok to keep searching.*

They waited, but nothing came. Rocktooth went in first, and Zander followed behind. The light from his scepter light up the stairway, showing it went up for many floors and down just one. *I'll try down this time.*

He opened the door, revealing what seemed to be a large kitchen. Many cans lay strewn about, ripped open, and the contents long since turned to dust. Next, He checked a linen closet, but all the material inside was rotted and moldy. Nothing was usable. Zander went inside. He gestured for Rocktooth to wait outside for him. The golem grumbled; Zander heard it in his head. He frowned at the golem, and Rocktooth looked away. Something scampered past him, and Zander aimed his staff at it, using a quick **[Arcane Bolt]** to kill it. *Just a rat,* He realized afterward.

Notification: You have killed a rat. +2 to experience and +1 Gold

Zander sighed in frustration. *Nothing yet, and I'm already super jumpy. Maybe Rocktooth was right. We're risking ourselves for nothing.* He was ready to call it and move to another floor of the Harrow when he caught sight of a thick iron door with some boxes placed in front of it. *I doubt anyone has been there before. What's behind that door?*

He directed Rocktooth to clear the boxes and opened the door. He found himself in a hallway leading further down. But the smell of something unnatural drifted on the air. *The Draugr.* He couldn't see far into the hallway and charged more magic into his staff, commanding it to form into a ball of light. **[Illuminate Sphere]**. The ball was pushed out from his staff and traveled down the hall. *If a Draugr had seen that, it would have attacked me already.*

The hallway was long and damp, made of concrete with a single door at its end. The smell of the Draugr drifted closer. *Rocktooth, close the door and watch my back. I'm going forward.* He could only hope that the summon could keep out the coming Draugr, even if all the golem did was brace the iron door.

Zander walked down the hall, and though the smell of the Draugr faded, the anxiety He was feeling hadn't. *Something is wrong here.* A chipped piece of the wall fell down, and Zander looked up, noticing for the first time the holes in the cement ceiling. The light of his illuminated the overhead body of a monster. *Far worse than a Draugr.*

It dropped to the ground in a humanish mass of spidery limbs, and Zander wasted no time in casting another [Arcane Bolt] before it could get up. The monster turned to her. Half of its face was gone, while the other was contorted into the grimacing face of a woman. *How long has it been up there in the dark?* The monster looked at him for a moment, curiously studying him as the monster salivated and licked its lips. At the far end of the hall, Rocktooth was no help, the golem was planted firmly in front of the door, and Zander could hear the banging of hungry Draugr on the other side. *There will be no escape that way.*

Zander pointed his staff again at the monster and used a spell He had seen the Elders of his village use. [Cleanse Abomination]. Amber light shot out of his staff directly at the monster. The effect was instant as it made a wheezing sound and collapsed on the floor.

He pointed the tip of his staff at the undead and said

a spell He had heard almost everyone who could do magic say. It was a simple, cleansing spell. The undead snarled at her; it made a wheezing sound like it was going to die again, and then it did.

Notification: You have killed a Darkling. +12 to experience, to 18 Gold.

Zander was looking at the body to see if it had only loot, when He heard another running towards him, He turned, but He was too late. It slammed into him, shoving him against something hard. He groaned. His side dragged with pain.

In the commotion, Zander didn't hear another of the monsters drop beside his until He stood face to face with another of the snarling abominations. This one was older than the last, weaker. One hand was gone entirely, and its entire face drooped uselessly. A clawed hand reached out, trying to tear at him, but Zander was able to get his staff in place to parry and moved past it.

It's too soon for another **[Cleanse Abomination]**. The monster howled, and the Draugr kept locked out by Rocktooth doubled their efforts, and Zander could see the door was starting to buckle. Pieces of both the door and Rocktooth were beginning to flake off from the strain.

Rocktooth, I'll summon you again. Zander told the golem through their connection as he charged a different spell through him and used a lesser ability. Bright light completely filled the room, blinding the monstrous female and the Draugr that were almost through the door. **[Flare]**. He slammed his staff into the stunned monster and ran past it, straight towards the door He had seen.

Relief flooded his body as the door opened easily enough. Without even waiting to see if the room was safe, He slammed it behind him, feeling an instant sense of gratification when He pulled an iron bar over the door, further securing it. His staff's light revealed a green circle, and Zander was drawn to it, compelled by it. He touched it. Overhead a row of electric lights turned on, revealing 12 pods. Each as cold as ice.

I need to get Rocktooth back here. Though he'd already used a lot of his magic, Zander knew better than to try and forge ahead without Rocktooth. He reached into a small pouch secured to the base of his staff and pulled out a small river stone, and set it on the ground, aiming the spell **[Summon Guardian]**. Within seconds, Rocktooth was revived, but the golem looked at him strangely as if to say, *Why did you call me back so so early.*

Guard the door Rocktooth, He commanded as He moved closer to the frozen pods. He held his staff, using an **[Scan]** on each. Only one showed any sign of life. He walked closer to the pod. The top surface was made of glass, revealing through the glass the face of a sleeping woman. The door started to thump, it wouldn't last much longer.

He jumped back. *An ancient. Here? A human!* He had not seen a human in a long time, not a live one anyway. Zander didn't know how to open the pod, so He smashed open the pod with his staff. It took six hits, in all, to reveal the blue hair of a woman within. He pulled her out and held her head in his hands as he used a **[Scan]** to check for life, or at least a strand of it remaining. Zander was sure he felt it. It was faint,

WOLFE LOCKE

but it was there. He closed his eyes and imagined the stream of mana within him, and this time, Zander channeled it all into the woman [**Heal**].

Notification: Class Unlocked - Necromancer
Details: Necromancers subvert the natural order of the land to raise their minions. Once the pathways of Necromancy have been unlocked, it cannot be forgotten and leaves those touched permanently changed.

Notification: New Minion Unlocked - The Frozen Dame
Details: ?????

Notification: Level Up! You are now level 16
Details: You have passed the 100 experience threshold to level up. You have earned +1 to Magic, +1 to Mana, and +2 to Health

Status – Zander - Level 16

Class – Necromancer

Race – Post-Human – Sub-Type Elven
Health, 40>41 Mana regen per hour, 18 Attack, 12 Defense, 39>40 Magic 16>17
Abilities:
Summon Monster -
*Golem – Mana Cost – 40 - Summons a Golem of Stone from the Netherworld to come to your aid. This summon is a permanent companion and has no time limit. It has 200 Health, 30 Defense, and 29 Attack. If destroyed, it can be resummoned once a day.

* Hawk – Mana Cost – 30 - Summons a Spirit Hark for 3 minutes that allows the summoners to see through the Hawk. After 3 minutes, the Hawk returns to the Netherworld. Has 20 Health, 3 Defense, and 1 attack.

* Summon Ice Dame - Mana Cost - 20 - ???

****

****

Chapter Two: Welcome! To the Future

The woman sat up with a start, frantically gasping for breath. She had blue skin and was covered in ice crystals, and Zander could feel the frost magic spilling off of her. He slowly moved away, trying not to startle her. She was still desperately struggling to inhale, almost choking as she fought for air.

"I don't think you need to breathe," he said gently. "You're undead."

"Undead?" she said. "That can't be true. I just fell asleep a few minutes ago."

Notification: You have gained a party member, Celeste.

Details: Found in a Cryopod, this ancient human has been reborn as a frost spirit bound to your service.

She looked down at herself and yelped in surprise. She tried to brush the frost off of her body. It didn't work.

"What's the last thing you remember?" Zander said.

Celeste frowned. "I was…I was fighting. We were in the city and…something bad was happening. I don't remember what it was. They were chasing us. Something. Inhuman. Dark things. I remember I turned—there was a little boy. My friends went on ahead, but I went back to save the little boy. He was crying. I was able to reach him, to touch his arm. And then, whatever was chasing us caught up. It got him first, then me. It was—"

She winced, remembering.

"—It was very bad."

"That sounds like the Harrowing," Zander said. "But doesn't explain how you ended up in the pod."

"The Harrowing?" She asked, the word and its meaning unfamiliar to her.

"I'll explain later." He replied. Zander knew this wasn't the time.

"Oh. I remember. When I woke up, the boy was gone. My friend Maxwell was carrying me on his back. He was running from something—from the same things that had been chasing us before. I was wounded, but still alive. He brought me into this building and sealed me into the pod. I think he hoped something like this would happen: that someone would find me in the future and heal me. As the pod sent me to sleep, I saw them break in. They killed Maxwell like they killed the little boy—"

"And now you've been resurrected," Zander said. "You're a frost spirit now. You're bound to my service —but in exchange, you can do powerful magic."

"Magic?" Celeste said, wrinkling her brow in confusion.

The door thumped again, more loudly this time, and started to splinter. Zander could hear the Draugr shrieking outside.

Enough talking, Rocktooth said, glaring at them. *We're going to have some action soon.*

"Let's hope you know how to use your new powers," Zander said, reaching for his own magic. "We're going to need them."

"Powers!" Celeste said. "I don't have any powers. I'm only human."

"I think you're a little bit more than that!" Zander said, gesturing at her blue, ice-covered body. "I trust you can figure it out!"

The Draugr smashed at the door again, and it splintered even further. Through the hole the monsters had created, Zander could see them milling about in the hallway outside. They were chittering to each other eagerly, and hungry for blood.

Here we go, Rocktooth boomed. *Are you ready?*

"Ready as we'll ever be!" Zander shouted.

He was worried. He'd already used a lot of his magic navigating the building, and resurrecting Celeste and binding her to him had drained him even more. He wasn't sure if he had it in him to fight off the Draugr swarm.

It seemed like every monster in the building had converged on the room, hoping to rip him and the undead woman apart with their teeth. This must have been why the Harrow had been so empty before. They had all been waiting down here in the depths, trying to draw him in.

Another blow widened the hole the monsters had already created, and the first of the Draugr shoved its head through. It was hideous, vaguely human in form but bloated with death and black with rot. One eyeball dangled down its cheek, leaking fluid. Its teeth were jagged and yellow, and its mouth was coated with blood and gore.

Glaring at him with its one remaining eye, the Draugr screamed and scrabbled at the door with its hands. Zander cast **[Arcane Bolt]** and it fell back. Almost immediately, another one took its place. He used **[Arcane Bolt]** again, blowing the new monster's head off, only for it to be replaced with yet another. More Draugr clustered behind it, pushing their way forward in mindless rage.

There are too many. He wasn't going to be able to pick them off one at a time like this. He'd be fully drained of his magic long before he was able to destroy all the Draugr. Worse, they were still smashing at the door. They could swarm them. The door wouldn't last much longer at this rate. There had to be another way.

As if on cue, another piece of the door splintered off, and the monsters started to push their way into the chamber. Their eyes were wild, and their mouths opened and closed relentlessly with an unholy hunger that could never be satiated.

"Rocktooth!" Zander shouted. "Your turn!"

The golem stepped forward obediently. *At your service.*

Rocktooth struck out violently with its smooth and powerful arms of stone, knocking three Draugr against the wall of the room. They shrieked and lay still, limbs contorted into unnatural positions from the force of the blow. Rocktooth held the line, smashing Draugr with its hands and crushing them beneath its feet. The monsters couldn't get past it—at least, for now.

Zander turned back to look at Celeste. She was cowering in a corner of the room, eyes wide with fear.

"Wha—what are those things?" she said, almost sobbing. "They look like the monsters that were chasing us back in—back before."

"They probably *are* the same monsters," Zander said. "Or similar ones. Draugr don't age like we do. Eventually they wear out, but only if they get attacked or injured."

"Draugr?"

"I *will* explain," Zander said. "I promise. But not right now. How's it going? Do you think you'll be able to work any frost magic soon?"

"Frost magic?" Celeste said, looking baffled. "I have no idea what you're talking about, I swear. I believe you when you say I *do* have that power, but I have no idea how to access it."

Zander hissed with frustration and looked back at Rocktooth. The golem was still doing well, but the gap in the door was widening and more Draugr were pushing their way through every second. It wasn't long before his summon would be overwhelmed.

"You need to figure it out!" Zander said. "I'm drained, and Rocktooth can only do so much! I resurrected you for this purpose!"

"Resurrected—me?"

A bloodcurdling shriek echoed through the chamber, and Zander's stomach dropped. Monsters of the Dark. He'd only seen the creatures once or twice in his life, and he'd always run from them immediately. The stories he'd heard from those who'd tried to fight them chilled his blood.

They were vicious and relentless creatures, reanimated corpses that had mutated into hideous forms. A Monster of the Dark, once aggravated, would stop at nothing until its opponents were dead on the ground and it was feasting on their flesh. And they were stuck with one in a doorless chamber, unable to escape.

Zander! Help!

Rocktooth was being swarmed by Draugr. The un-dead creatures couldn't hurt a rock golem much, but they were driving it back. They piled on top of it and tried to knock it to the ground, and it staggered, almost dropping to one knee. His summon needed help, and it needed it now.

"Rocktooth! Duck!" Zander said.The same awful shriek rang out again, closer this time, and it was answered by a matching one from further down the dungeon. The Monster of the Dark was calling to its allies, telling them there was a feast to be had here. That was very bad news.

He couldn't do anything about the Monster just yet, but he could at least help the golem. He whipped his staff around and pointed it at two Draugr that had leaped onto Rocktooth's back and were trying fruit-lessly to bite through its stone hide. **[Arcane Bolt]** dis-patched them both.

Rocktooth stumbled around the chamber, ripping Draugr off of itself, as Zander used his magic to help. The number of undead outside the door was reach-ing a critical mass, though. The situation was getting very dangerous.

"Any luck?" Zander shouted back to Celeste, but she only shook her head. He groaned. *What was the point of bringing back an undead frost spirit if she couldn't control her own powers?*

"Well," he said. "If any of them get close to you, don't let them bite you. You'll become one of them, and that's the last thing we need!"

The awful shriek of the Monster of the Dark sounded again, very close this time, and the Draugr all froze, jaws slack with confusion, vacant eyes darting in all directions. They dropped off of Rocktooth's back in unison and backed away against the sides of the chamber, chittering.

Get ready, Rocktooth said, voice booming in Zander's head. *It's coming.*

"*They're* coming," Zander replied. "I'm almost sure there are two."

The horrifying, meaty slap of half-rotten flesh dragging against stone echoed through the chamber as the Monster approached. The Draugr cringed back against the wall.

One by one, the Monster's spindly arms gripped the doorframe. It was a modified corpse, six legged and naked, with a hideous man-like head. Its mouth was a gaping slash across his face, augmented with razor-sharp and rotting teeth. It screamed, and its breath smelled like carrion.

Immediately behind it came the second Monster. This one had only two legs and a long meaty tail. It dragged its body along behind it with its forepaws. The upper half of its face was human, but the bottom half decayed into a mess of tentacles that looked like hanging intestines.

They screamed to each other, clearly making a plan. Then, they turned to face Rocktooth and Zander. The Monsters advanced together, forming an impenetrable wall of flesh. Their hungry maws gaped, and their eyes burned with unquenchable rage.

Zander fired **[Arcane Bolt]** after **[Arcane Bolt]** but the Monsters were completely unfazed. He tried **[Cleanse Abomination]**, but he was running low on power. The lead Monster sneezed once, spraying them with viscous black phlegm, but otherwise the spell had no effect. Rocktooth tried to beat them back with his massive arms, but they ignored him and pressed forward relentlessly.

Emboldened, the Draugr moved away from the wall and joined the Monsters in their attack. They lurched forward, gibbering eagerly at the prospect of the feast ahead.

"Celeste!" Zander screamed. "Now's the time! Now or never!"

But there was no response.

Zander tried to fire another **[Arcane Bolt]**, but he was tapped out. The Monsters were less than two feet away now. He flinched as their sharp teeth drew close to his face. At least Rocktooth might get out of this all right, even if he didn't.

There was a loud noise, as if a massive window had shattered into a thousand shards of glass, and a flickering blue light filled the chamber. The Draugr and Monsters of the Dark fell back, shrieking. Zander turned, wonderstruck, to see Celeste standing tall behind him, glowing with ethereal power. Her eyes radiated their own internal light—a vivid electric blue.

"You figured it out!" he said. "A bit late, but just in time!"

She nodded and gestured at the nearest Draugr. **[Ice Bolt]** shot from her hands, freezing it in place on the spot. Rocktooth roared, re-invigorated, and smashed four Draugr to the ground—two with each arm.

"Rocktooth!" Zander shouted. "Let's clear the way for her! We get the Draugr, she gets the Monsters!"

Understood. I'll do my best. The golem responded.

Celeste also nodded a confirmation, and the three

warriors turned to face the undead together, as one. A united front.

A globe of glowing ice formed in her hands, and she shot it at the six-legged Monster with a jubilant grin. It screeched and recoiled, crushing several Draugr as it did. Dark ichor oozed from a hole in its side. It was grievously wounded, but not dead.

Celeste advanced on it and shot it again and again as it tried and failed to attack her. It was covered in ice, almost frozen solid, but it stubbornly kept trying to snap at her. Finally, she honed her frost magic into a thick, razor-sharp icicle and buried it in the beast's throat. It choked, clawing at the weapon with its useless front paws, trying and failing to pull it out of its neck. Finally, it lay still. Celeste stood next to it, one hand still on the icicle, stunned and proud.

Meanwhile, Zander and Rocktooth went in on the Draugr. Rocktooth churned their brittle limbs into pulp, while Zander drew on the last of his strength to blast their heads in with **[Arcane Blast]**. The Draugr tried to grab at them, but their resistance was useless and feeble. Slowly but surely, without the threat of the Monsters of the Dark, they were clearing out the chamber.

Celeste was still standing next to the Monster she'd killed, staring at it in shock.

"Take on the other Monster, Celeste!" Zander said.

She jumped, suddenly coming back to herself. "Right! Right! The other Monster!"

It was slithering behind her, groaning with fury, beady eyes focused on its dead companion. The tentacles dribbled from its mouth, looking raw and disgusting in the eerie blue light that emanated from Celeste's magical form. She clapped her hands together and got to work just as it lunged at her. Its tentacles tried to wrap themselves around her arms.

"Help!" she shouted.

Zander turned and shot a quick **[Arcane Blast]** at the creature's head. It squealed and rolled over on its side. Two tentacles dropped to the ground. Regrouping, Celeste raised another globe of ice into her hands. She directed **[Ice Blades]** at the monster, burying it beneath a massive barrage of ice shards. It tried to roll out of the way, but it was too slow and ungainly. Ichor dripped from a thousand wounds all over the creature's body as it slumped to the ground. Its fat tentacles went slack, and it gave one final shudder and died.

The Monsters were dead, but the room was still full of Draugr. Zander and Rocktooth were working to destroy them, but it was taking too long. They were running out of power, and Rocktooth's movements were getting slower and slower. Celeste pressed her hands together and concentrated. Frost filled the room, covering the floor with ice. The Draugr froze solid and shattered into pieces, leaving the allies alone in the chamber, victorious.

"You did it!" Zander said, feeling inordinately proud of her. "That was amazing."

"I—I—wow," she said, looking woozy. "Was that magic?"

The light slowly dimmed out of the chamber as her frost form left her. Her eyes went dark and rolled back in her head, and she collapsed to the ground in a dead faint

If you want to read similarly styled books, check out LitRPG Books, Fantasy Nation, and GameLit Society on Facebook to connect with other readers and authors.

LitRPG Releases does a decent job at putting out new titles to check out.

Lastly, join the LitRPG Guild at
Link: **https://www.facebook.com/groups/ litrpgguild**
Or on -- Discord Link: https://discord.gg/YGtjN8r

"To learn more about LitRPG, talk to authors in-cluding myself, and just have an awesome time, please join the LitRPG Group."

Printed in Great Britain
by Amazon